COLTER SONS BOOK 3

THE RAILROAD MAGNATE

Karen Baney

desert life
media

The Railroad Magnate: Colter Sons Book 3
By Karen Baney

Publisher:
Desert Life Media, LLC
Gilbert, AZ 85295

www.karenbaney.com

Printed in the United States of America

ISBN-979-8-9863369-1-6

Thus says the Lord:
"Cursed is the man who trusts in man
and makes flesh his strength,
whose heart turns away from the Lord.
He is like a shrub in the desert,
and shall not see any good come.
He shall dwell in the parched places of
the wilderness,
in an uninhabited salt land.

"Blessed is the man who trusts in the
Lord, whose trust is the Lord.
He is like a tree planted by water,
that sends out its roots by the stream,
and does not fear when heat comes,
for its leaves remain green,
and is not anxious in the year of
drought, for it does not cease to bear
fruit."

—Jeremiah 17:5-8

CHAPTER I

My name is James Colter, the first-born son of the Colter family. Unlike my brothers, my position in the family never crosses my mind. Which of my siblings holds the highest regard in my parents' eyes matters little to me. I know they love and respect me. My career and ambition take far greater space in my thoughts.

An entrepreneurial spirit runs deep in my family. My papa had it, but me? My drive and ambition are twice what Papa's ever was.

Will Colter, my papa, built a successful enterprise outside of Prescott as the first rancher in the area. When settlers started arriving in 1864, the year before I was born, he saw an opportunity to take some of his cattle, butcher it, and provide meat to the new town. That was when the Colter Meat Company was born.

As more settlers moved to town and when the Army set up Fort Whipple, Papa wrote to my Uncle Adam, asking if he'd like to start a horse training and breeding company. He wasn't my uncle then. He later married Aunt Julia when I was little, so they've always been Uncle Adam and Aunt Julia to me.

Anyway, after that was the end of Papa's entrepreneurial

aspirations.

Me? Well, I'm just getting started and I have no intention of ever stopping.

There are two days in my life that changed me forever. The first was when I was fourteen. In November 1879, the South-ern Pacific Railroad broke ground in Arizona City, which is now called Yuma. By Christmastime, the news reached our small town. I instantly fell in love when I saw the train engine in the newspaper. My plan to become a railroad magnate took shape. I only needed to be in the right place at the right time.

To secure my future goals, I made it clear I would not assume the responsibilities of the ranch despite Papa's desire. It took a lot of persuading. Thankfully, my brother Sam excelled at all aspects of ranching.

As soon as I was able, I moved to Tucson and worked for the Southern Pacific until I climbed my way to a managerial position. After leaving that job as the Superintendent of Trans-portation, I moved back to Prescott for a similar role with Bullock's Central Arizona Railway. By the age of twenty-three, I received a promotion to Vice President of Transpor-tation, earning more money than I dreamed possible. My mentor, Frank Murphy, joined forces with a local mine owner to start a competing railroad out of Prescott in 1890. Being a mover and shaker, I joined him in a comparable role, bringing some capital funds with me. I was well on my way to accomplishing my dreams.

Like I said, there were two days that changed my life forever. The second one? Well, that's the whole point of this story.

CHAPTER 2

Prescott, Arizona Territory
May 27, 1891

JAMES

My job at a railroad as the Vice President of Transportation kept me busy at the expense of my social life. Last fall, I left my job at Bullock's railroad, and I joined Frank Murphy's fledgling venture. Our goal was to build a new, shorter line that connected with the Atlantic & Pacific in Ash Fork. The new railroad route would extend from Ash Fork to Prescott to Congress, Wickenburg, and on into Phoenix, the new capital of the territory, much further south than Bullock's line.

Two days prior we officially incorporated the Santa Fe, Prescott, & Phoenix Railway, though our plans and investments started long before then. By the start of our railroad, we raised four million dollars, a staggering sum for the day, though far short of the cost to run the Southern Pacific Railroad through southern Arizona over fifteen years prior. Railroad construction was perhaps the most expensive venture known to man. Tax exemptions and incentives from the governor made it more palatable. Frankly, if railroads had not promised to significantly reduce the cost of shipping ore from the area mines, I doubted any man would champion them.

My job satisfied me. I loved being in the middle of everything, from planning and logistics to construction, fundraising, and operations. I had every confidence Frank Murphy and the President, D.B. Robinson, who came over from the Atlantic & Pacific, would make our new line a success. With my help, of course.

That day was the celebration of the birth of our new railroad: the Santa Fe, Prescott, & Phoenix Railway. I donned my most expensive black suit, red silk vest, red neck scarf, and bowler hat. Then I grabbed my dark wood walking stick before I walked from my home in Prescott to the ballroom hosting the celebration.

As I entered the ballroom, my eyes snagged on a heavenly creature and my pulse picked up pace. Her dark brown hair complimented her ivory skin. Her sapphire blue dress brought out the vibrancy of her blue eyes, which beckoned to me from across the room. Stunning.

Before I formed a conscious thought, I walked across the ballroom to her. Her beauty became more apparent as I approached. Her curves filled out the dress nicely. My heart thudded in my chest. She was a stranger to me, and I resolved to meet her. I ignored all my responsibilities as the Vice President, and I did not stop until I stood before her. The music started, so I extended my hand toward her.

"May I have this dance?" I asked.

Pink tinged her cheeks as she placed her delicate hand on mine and stood. Everything about her exuded softness and femininity. She was only a few inches shorter than me, which I liked. My eyes locked with hers as I pulled her close. She smelled like roses and vanilla. Her long brown hair trailed down her back. It tickled my hand as I placed it on her trim waist.

At that moment, there was no one else in the room. Just her.

My feet glided across the dance floor. As I led us in a waltz, she kept perfect pace with me. Then she smiled and my heart danced even faster than my feet. The first dance sped by without a word exchanged between us.

As the second dance started, I asked, "How have we not met before now?"

"Oh, but we may have." Pink colored her cheeks. Her dark lashes fluttered as she looked down for a moment, stealing my breath away.

"I'm certain I would have remembered you." One side of my mouth curved up.

"You are James Colter, are you not?"

She knew who I was. That did not surprise me. My reputation in the community often proceeded me. Everyone knew I was a railroad magnate and a man who accomplished great things for our town.

"Indeed. And you are?"

"Keri Glassman."

As I maintained a steady lock on her mesmerizing eyes, I led her for a third dance. "Miss Glassman. Of the Alex Glassman family?"

"Yes, he is my father."

That surprised me. I didn't know he had such a lovely and charming daughter. "And you believe we've met before?"

The sound of her soft laughter endeared her to me even more.

"I know it."

I flashed her a saucy grin. "Really?"

"I am rarely wrong."

Confident. Sure. And beautiful. I wondered where she had been all my life.

"Care to remind me where we met before?"

"You have a reputation, Mr. Colter, for being a very astute man. I am certain you will solve the mystery all on your own without my assistance."

Her laughter floated in the air as I spun her around. Then I gently guided her back to me. I returned my hand to her waist.

"Did I meet you at your parents' law office?"

She shook her head and smiled.

The next song picked up the pace. My footwork matched the rhythm, and we breezed across the dance floor. I could no longer discern if my heart palpitated because of her attention or the brisk tempo of our dance.

"Where then? Tell me."

I spun her again. That time, when she returned to me, I held her closer. She grew breathless and her lips drew my gaze. For the first time in my life, I wondered if I had been missing someone like her. I cleared my throat and forced my eyes back to hers.

"Congratulations," she said. "Starting a new railroad is quite an accomplishment."

"Thank you."

"I know the local businessmen, ranchers, and farmers will appreciate a more reliable railroad."

My chest puffed under her praise as the music slowed. I held her close to my chest with my face only a few inches from hers. I could almost feel her heart beating in rhythm with mine.

As she looked over my shoulder, she stiffened and drew

back. I wiped away a frown when a man stood next to us.

"May I cut in?" Her father's direct eye contact told me I had only one choice.

Then I reluctantly released the charming Miss Keri Glassman. "Pleasure to see you, Miss Glassman."

Her eyes followed me as I joined my colleagues at the head table. Once I sat down, I watched her with her father. She glanced at me several times, which caused a strange feeling in my stomach. I liked it.

The party continued for hours as I ate and drank with the other officers of the railroad. We congratulated each other for incorporating the railroad and discussed the promise it held for our future and the future of Prescott.

I lost track of Miss Glassman and missed her departure. Though disappointed, I thought I might call on her. I knew the location of her family's home.

Those blue eyes haunted my dreams for some time, yet I never followed through. I forgot about her as my job consumed my time.

———

KERI

When James Colter entered the ballroom, I smiled. Years passed since I had seen him as a little girl out on Grandpa Larson's ranch. He looked even more handsome than I remembered.

As if my thoughts summoned him, he walked directly toward me, which surprised both me and my parents. Papa's client invited us to the party to celebrate the launch of the Santa Fe, Prescott, & Phoenix Railway. He helped secure several connections and contracts.

I thought it was an illusion that James's steps directed his path toward me. Certainly, he would veer off to some other woman at any moment. When he didn't and he appeared before me, I failed to seek Papa's permission, and I gave my hand to him.

When I rose to my feet, his gaze warmed me. He pulled me close and led me in a waltz. He stood slightly taller than me and I was grateful, as I thought myself too tall for a young woman. Yet, in his arms, my height did not bother me. His brown eyes never strayed from mine unless I broke the contact. His dark hair slicked to one side. The suit he wore trumpeted his wealth and success.

My cheeks heated as he twirled me around and spoke with me. My heart raced as I enjoyed his attention and the feel of his hand touching my waist. I knew my conversation appeared coy. Still, I relished his focused attention as we danced. Somehow, me, the reserved teenager, captured and kept his attention on the dance floor.

I lost track of how many songs we danced to. It was him and me. I hoped to dance with him all night.

Unfortunately, Papa had other ideas. He stepped in and finished a dance with me before he escorted me back to our table. As we ate our meal, I did not take part in the conversation. Instead, I watched James at his table at the front of the room. He laughed. He spoke with confidence to his peers. More than once, he looked my way, which made my heart flutter.

When Papa stood and announced it was time to retire for the night, I stuffed back my disappointment. I had hoped for just one more breathtaking dance with James.

The walk home filled with tension as Mama scolded Papa.

"She's only sixteen. He's a good ten years older than her."

Papa laughed. "Unlike you and me?"

I held back a giggle. My papa was nine years older than my mama, a fact which Mama seemed to forget in the conversation about me and James.

"Mel, it was only a dance," he said. "I doubt we'll see him soon."

Mama frowned. "It was six dances. Six. She is too young for him."

As Papa tucked Mama's hand into the crook of his arm, he rested his hand over hers. He said nothing further the rest of the way home.

When I retired to my room, I dreamed of those dances with James, his handsome face, his witty banter, and how he made me feel special. Thoughts of him filled my mind in the following weeks until, slowly over time, the magical night of dancing faded to a distant memory.

CHAPTER 3

November 10, 1891

KERI

"I need to head up to Chicago with Frank Murphy," Papa announced at supper one night.

"When do you need to leave?" Mama asked.

"Two days."

Mama's shoulders sagged. "Too bad I'm in the middle of a trial. I'd love to go." She was the Larson in the Larson & Glassman law firm. She used her maiden name as she practiced law.

Papa smiled sympathetically.

"I could go," I said without thinking.

Papa rubbed his long beard and raised an eyebrow Mama's direction.

"I don't know," Mama hesitated. "Chicago is a big city. Who knows how rough it could be?"

"Relax, Mel. We aren't sending her off on her own. She'll be with me the entire time."

Mama pushed her food around on her plate as she frowned.

"If Frank is successful, I'll have several lengthy contracts to review. You know I could use Keri's eye for detail."

Even though I was sixteen, I hoped Mama would allow me to miss school. Last summer, I worked at my parents' law firm and learned enough to help Papa in Chicago. I bit my lower lip as my excitement grew. If only Mama would consent.

"But you'll miss Thanksgiving," Mama said.

Papa took her hand and squeezed it. "Let this year be the exception. We'll be back long before Christmas."

"Alright."

I squealed. I was going to Chicago. It would be the adventure of my young life.

On November sixteenth, we arrived in Chicago. The city bustled with activity. We took a carriage from the train station to the Palmer House downtown. The beautiful brick building spread out from the corner of Chicago Street and State Street. The corner of the building was rounded and capped with a gothic-styled dome. I counted the rows of windows and estimated the building was seven stories tall.

The ornate architecture of the exterior barely did the opulence of the interior justice. Marble and gold gilded nearly every surface. The lobby sparkled and glowed like what I imagined a castle of old might.

As Papa led me into the dining room, my breath left me. A large twenty-four carat gold and crystal chandelier lit the entire room. The magnificent chandelier was nearly ten feet tall. Polished dark wood pillars drew my eye up to the fresco-painted transom ceiling.

"Keri." Papa's words drew me out of the trance. I took his arm as he guided me to a large table with several men from the railroad.

James Colter smiled as he stood and took my hand. "Miss

Glassman. A pleasure to see you again."

My face warmed, and I was glad he remembered me. As I smiled and offered a soft greeting, I studied his appearance. He looked handsome in his black suit. Those brown eyes. I could stare into them all night long.

"Gentlemen, this is my daughter, Keri."

I tore my gaze away from James as Papa introduced me to Frank Murphy, who I recognized from the dance in May. The other men were executives and lawyers for the Atlantic & Pacific Railroad.

When I took a seat across from James, he smiled at me.

"How have you been?" he asked.

"Well enough. I'm thrilled to be here. The hotel is quite spectacular."

"Not nearly as gorgeous as you."

My eyes dropped to my plate as my cheeks warmed. In that moment, I was twice as grateful to Mama for letting me join Papa on the trip.

Throughout the meal, James's gaze connected with mine, which reminded me of our dances in May. I enjoyed listening to him talk about the railroad business and I thought I could listen to his tenor voice all night.

However, after two hours, my eyes drooped, and I stifled a yawn, but not before he noticed.

"It's getting late, and the lovely Miss Glassman traveled all day. Perhaps we should adjourn for the evening?"

The men agreed.

Papa led me to our suite, which was as ostentatious as the rest of the hotel. I looked out the window at the gas-lit streets. They glowed yellow and gave the street a homey feel.

I yawned again before I walked into my bedroom as I unwound my long hair and brushed it until it shone. Then I loosely braided it and fell into the fluffy, warm bed. Dreams of a young princess dancing with her prince in a golden palace sweetened my sleep.

———

JAMES

The moment I saw Keri Glassman in the dining room, I remembered our dance from May. That night had crossed my mind often, though my work overshadowed the memory.

My pulse sped up as I watched her. She wore a lovely pale green dress lined with ivory lace. Her mesmerizing blue eyes sparkled as the chandelier cast a radiance on her soft skin. I could hardly believe my fortune that Alex brought her to Chicago. The thought of spending time alone with her pleased me.

Though she said little during the meal, my gaze often connected with hers. Each time it did, her soft cheeks bloomed with rosy circles. My, she held some unexplainable power over me. Her presence brought me joy and when she left for her room, the evening seemed less exciting.

I sighed and scolded myself for pining over her. My purpose in Chicago had nothing to do with her and everything to do with securing a contract with the A&P to ship goods from their line's junction in Ash Fork down to Prescott and further south when our line completed in the coming years.

When I grew weary of the glad-handing, I retired to my room. An unfamiliar pang rooted in my soul. Loneliness. I could not recall feeling it prior to that moment. My job kept me far too busy to realize I was alone. Work plans and problems consumed my thoughts, and my mind never saved space for many feelings.

The strange feeling nagged me as I sipped on a brandy in the privacy of my room. I didn't know what it meant and reminded myself I was there for work. I did not need any distractions. When I finished the brandy, I went to bed.

The next morning, I woke early. Once I dressed in a light gray suit with a navy neck scarf, I made my way down to the dining room for breakfast. Frank greeted me, so I sat with him. Within minutes, Alex and Keri Glassman joined us.

"What is on the agenda?" Alex asked.

"We'll head over to the A&Ps office after breakfast," Frank said. "I must apologize, but we have no one to escort your daughter around the city."

Alex said, "She's here to work with me. She has an excelent eye for the details in contracts. I'd like to take credit for mentoring her, but that is a God-given talent."

The apples of her cheeks flushed pink under her father's compliment.

I smiled. Not only was she lovely, but she was also quite intelligent. Both attributes intrigued me.

"Alright. Hopefully, our business discussion won't bore you," Frank said.

"Not at all. I find the details of the railroad business quite fascinating," she said with confidence.

The carriage ride to the office was extremely pleasant. Keri sat directly across from me. I watched as she took in the sights of the city. Awe and curiosity flitted across her features. Each time she glanced my way, I smiled.

During the first day of meetings, we barely set the groundwork for the contract negotiations. It would take several days to cover the topics of equipment, traffic, and schedules. Keri took copious notes and listened intently. She seemed to pick up certain details, which made me wonder what she perceived, and I missed.

After the long day, we freshened up before heading down to the dining room. That evening, she wore a fetching yellow dress that glowed like the sun against the backdrop of the glittering dining room. I held out a chair for her before I sat across from her again.

"Did we bore you?" I asked, searching for some topic of conversation so I could hear her sweet voice.

"Not at all. It sounded like the A&P is amiable to negotiations."

"Yes, Frank is a persuasive man."

Frank snorted. "I can't take all the credit. James has done as much to set the stage as I have. Besides, the A&P is weary of working with Bullock."

"That is no surprise," Alex said. "He seems to make some unusual decisions. And he has failed to deliver on the southern route. Now that Phoenix is the new capital, that line will become critical to the growth of the territory."

"Exactly," I agreed. "Growth of industry and the population means increased opportunity for our line and for the A&P. As they get to know us this week, I'm certain we'll be able to come up with a firm agreement."

"With the two of you watching our legal backs, I'm confident," Frank said.

The next few days flew by, and we agreed to table negotiations over the weekend.

On Saturday, I found myself restless and eager to leave the confines of the hotel. I headed to the lobby where I found Keri sitting on a Victorian chair. Her father sat nearby as he read the newspaper.

"Good morning," I greeted them. Impulsively, I asked, "Would you care to join me to view the construction of the World's Fair?"

"I thought that was closed to the public," Alex said.

"Not when one has friends in the right places," I bragged.

"Papa, can I go?"

Alex folded the paper and set it aside.

"Please? Aren't the Colters and Grandpa Larson long-time family friends? Certainly, you can trust James to escort me with decorum."

I held back a smile, since it would be detrimental to her argument. I found her negotiating skills impressive.

Alex sighed. "Alright. You may go. I hope to see you for supper."

She stood and kissed his cheek. "Thank you, Papa."

Then I helped Keri into her fur coat. She placed a hand on my arm as I led her to a waiting carriage. The driver stopped at a spot overlooking the construction.

"When is it supposed to open?" she asked as I helped her down from the carriage.

"I believe it is supposed to open on Columbus Day 1892. That would mark the four-hundredth anniversary of Colum-bus's arrival in America."

I stood next to her as we looked over the transformation of Jackson Park. Canals and water channels snaked through the park. The rough steel frame of several buildings dotted the landscape. The lack of walls allowed us to see through their skeletons.

"Too bad we couldn't walk through the park," she said. "It must be amazing to stand in the middle of a building. I'm certain they feel expansive."

"I'm sure they do."

I unfolded a copy of a sketch of the plans from my pocket and held it up in front of her. Then I pointed to the railroad lines. "That is the location of the terminal."

When she leaned closer, I could smell her perfume. Sweet and classy, like her. Never had I enjoyed the company of a woman so much.

She glanced at the paper. "How many lines will there be?"

"Dozens. Right now, the completed lines deliver construct-ion supplies."

As she studied the scene before her, I watched her excited gaze. She pointed to the paper, then to one of the steel skeletons.

"That must be the Administration Building. And that's the Mines & Mining Building."

"I think you're right."

We stood there for nearly an hour as we guessed what each depression in the ground would become.

"Can you imagine what it will look like when it's done?" she asked. As she turned to me, her eyes sparkled with life. The way she looked at me made me feel like I was someone rather special, causing my pulse to quicken.

"I can bring you back when it's done," I volunteered, without thinking through the implications.

She laughed. "I would like that, but I won't hold you to it since it's a long time from now."

My throat went dry as I studied her face. Rosy circles tinged her cheeks, likely from the cold air. Her lips looked red and inviting. As I remembered her comment about the Colters and Larsons, I cleared my throat.

Thinking she must be cold, I escorted her back to the carriage. The driver handed us an extra blanket, which I wrapped around her. My nervousness increased as the carriage started back toward the hotel.

"So, you're a Larson? George's granddaughter?"

"Yes. The ranch is where you first met me, though I doubt you paid any attention to me as a little girl. I was fairly young when you left."

I shook my head. "I suppose not."

The sound of the horse's hooves clopped along the cobble-stone street.

"Just how old are you?" I asked.

"Sixteen."

I hid my surprise as my shoulders slumped. She was too young. Ten years younger than me. No wonder her father stepped in at the dance.

For the rest of our trip, I avoided spending time alone with Keri, though she was at every meeting and every dinner. I reminded myself that I had no time for a social life. Once we returned to Prescott, she would forget about me, and I would forget about her. I hoped.

CHAPTER 4

KERI

We missed Thanksgiving, though the Palmer House prepared an elaborate spread of traditional food. Our time in Chicago wound down.

On the Saturday after Thanksgiving, Papa took me to the A&P office. It was the first weekend we worked. Their attorn-ey had several contracts drawn up.

Papa and I pored over the details.

"Papa," I said as I flipped through my notes, "I don't re-call a discussion about the SFP&P retaining fifty-eight per-cent of stock for five years *after* construction completes."

He searched through his notes. "You're right. I see noth-ing in my notes either."

Papa frowned when I pointed to the line in the contract.

"I'll get Frank and James."

While Papa was gone, I found the spot in my notes. The SFP&P expected to take at least three years to complete con-struction. It would tie up two million three hundred thou-sand dollars for at least eight years. I doubted that Frank and James were fine with that.

When they returned, Papa asked me to read the clause

for them.

"Fifty-eight percent is steep," Frank said.

I watched as James looked up and to his right. "If we get it down to fifty-one percent, it will reduce the amount to two million. That'd free up another three hundred thousand."

Frank tapped his fingers on the table. "Still feels a little steep. We may need to raise additional capital."

"Perhaps," I said. "They did agree to pay five percent of the interchange traffic in Ash Fork."

"Ah," James said. "I see what you are thinking. The sooner we finish the Ash Fork interchange, even if the line to Prescott is not done, the sooner we'll receive funds from the A&P."

I nodded, and Papa smiled, the pride clear in his eyes.

"Alex," Frank said, "get them down to fifty-one percent."

As Papa left the room, James sat down next to me. "Let me see what they settled on for the schedules."

I handed him the paper. Then I continued reading through the contract. The rest of it lined up with my notes. After James handed me the schedule back, I compared it as well.

When Papa returned, he gave me a side hug. "You saved us three hundred thousand dollars with your sharp eye."

After another hour, all parties signed the contract. Satisfaction filled me. I contributed to one of the most important contracts for our hometown in its brief history. That was the moment I decided I would become a contract attorney.

At supper that night, we celebrated the signed deal. The men slapped each other on the back and downed a great deal of brandy.

As the evening wore on, I stood. Papa and James stood

instantly. The other men were slower to rise.

"If you'll excuse me, gentlemen. Congratulations on a successful deal."

"I can escort you," James said.

Papa refused his offer and accompanied me to our room. Once I was safely inside, he returned to the dining room. I never heard him when he came back.

For the next few days, Papa and I took in the sights of the city before we returned home. The trip back home took three days on the train.

When we returned from Chicago, Papa no longer made me go to school. Instead, he convinced Mama to let me work in the law office with them, as I would learn far more under their mentoring.

———

Over the next year, Papa took on additional clients, so my workload increased. I conducted much of the research for his cases, and I reviewed contracts for both him and Mama. They hired another junior associate because of the influx of clients. I was so busy starting my career, I rarely thought of James.

One day in October 1892, Papa read the headline at break-fast: "World's Fair Opening Delayed."

My thoughts immediately went to James and the time we spent at the construction site in Chicago over a year prior. I remembered his casual promise to see it.

"When will it open?" I asked.

"May first of next year."

"How long will it be open?"

"It says here, the fair will be open from May through October."

"Can I go?" I asked.

Papa sighed. "I don't know. That's a long trip. The firm has more work than we can handle."

"I can take on more," I said.

"I thought you wanted to focus on contract work?" Mama asked.

I hesitated. I did. But I also wanted to see the World's Fair. "I do."

"We've talked about this," Papa said. "You are taking over contracts to prepare you for a position with the railroad, if they'll hire you."

"Do you really think they will hire a woman attorney?" my younger brother Clinton asked, which earned him a glare from Mama.

"What?" Archie asked. "Not everyone is as open-minded as Papa."

"We'll talk about the fair later," Papa said.

Despite Papa's dismissal, I resolved to make it to the World's Fair.

CHAPTER 5

October 10, 1892

KERI

"Alex," Papa's secretary said, "James Colter is here to see you. He apologized for not making an appointment. An urgent matter has come up."

"Show him in."

It had been a long time since I'd seen James. My heart rate sped up as I stood and smoothed out my skirt.

"Stay, Keri," Papa said. "I'm sure this will be an excellent learning opportunity."

As James entered Papa's office, I touched my hand to my hair and took a steadying breath. He looked quite dashing in his black suit and silver vest with a matching neck scarf.

"Miss Glassman," he greeted me. His smile was broad and sent my heart fluttering.

"Mr. Colter. A pleasure to see you again," I replied as I closed the door. I took a seat next to him across from Papa's large dark wood desk.

"How long has it been?"

Eleven months, one week, and three days. I surprised

myself that I knew the precise time. "A little over eleven months."

Papa laughed. "I'm sure if you asked her the number of days, she would know."

"Three hundred and forty-five days."

James chuckled. "You look well."

Heat warmed my cheeks. "Thank you."

After James took a deep breath, he turned his attention to Papa. "I need your help with a somewhat delicate case." His earlier joviality disappeared. "I will understand if you decline to help on this one."

"What makes you think I would decline?" Papa said.

James coughed. "It is a lawsuit against Colter Ranch."

Papa frowned, and I held my breath. Grandpa still owned part of the ranch.

"Unfortunately, my brother, Sam, is suing us because the tracks will go through a small section of the northwest corner of the ranch's land."

James handed Papa a sheet of paper.

"Even though we have the right-of-way from the territory, Sam is disputing it."

James held out another stack of papers for Papa. Papa handed me the first one as he took the stack. Then he scanned the brief.

"It says the suit is by all the partners of the ranch: Will Colter, Sam Colter, and George Larson," Papa said as he set the papers down. "Warren Cahill isn't a part of the suit?"

"No. Sam bought out his shares a few months ago. Warren moved his family down to Congress to start a ranch there. You can see why I would understand if you declined to represent us in this matter."

I frowned. Papa was Grandpa George's attorney. He had been since long before I was born. I could not imagine

Grandpa would be pleased to have Papa representing the SFP&P against him.

My eyes scanned the paper from the territory. It was iron clad. The territory granted the SFP&P, as a critical part of the transportation infrastructure, the right to take the disputed land.

"Is there no way to take another route?" I asked.

James shook his head. "The geology of the area leaves little wiggle room for that section of track. Boone and his team of surveyors went to great lengths to make sure the line goes through the smallest section of Colter land as possible."

I handed the right-of-way paper back to Papa. "I don't see how they can dispute this and win."

"Mel will not be happy," Papa said. "But I will represent you."

"Excellent. Here's the survey report from Boone, as well as a map of the disputed land. The case goes to trial in two days."

As James stood, he smiled at me. "Good to see you again, despite the circumstances."

"Agreed." I smiled as Papa stood and escorted James out of the office.

As soon as Papa came back, we discussed the case in more detail and strategized for the trial.

Papa said, "Please let me handle telling your mother about this. She won't be pleased, and I'd rather be the one to break the news."

I agreed.

Tension zinged in the air between my parents at supper. Fortunately, by the next morning, Mama seemed in a better mood.

Papa and I spent the day reviewing all the paperwork

regarding the case and mapped out our plan for witnesses. We met with James and let him know Boone needed to be available during the trial to speak as an expert on the surveying report.

———

JAMES

I was relieved that Alex took the case. I knew it put him in an awkward position with his father-in-law and his wife. Truth be told, I was in a fair amount of hot water with my father and brother. Had I not been an officer of the SFP&P, I doubted they would have sued. I was certain their attorney, Seth Rankin, advised them against it. At least that was what Boone's wife, Jaclyn, let slip on my last visit to their surveying office.

When I entered the courtroom, Papa and George sat in the first row of the gallery behind Seth Rankin and Sam. I went over and greeted them with a smile. I wanted to clarify that I would harbor no ill-will because of the case. Papa and George greeted me warmly. Sam frowned and refused to shake my hand.

I took a seat next to Keri and Alex. Boone sat in the first row of the gallery behind us.

"How was your reception?" Boone asked as he leaned forward.

"Not bad, except for Sam."

He grunted as the judge entered the courtroom.

Once we took our seats again, the court clerk announced the case. The judge allowed Rankin to speak first. Then Alex stood and gave his opening remarks.

"During this trial, I will show that my client, the Santa Fe, Prescott, & Phoenix Railway, took appropriate measures to keep the impact to Colter Ranch as small as possible. My client petitioned to the territory for the right-of-way. They granted it and the railway route falls within that right-of-way."

When it was our turn to present information, Alex said, "We'd like to call Boone Colter to the stand."

"Colter?" the judge asked.

"Yes, your honor. Boone Colter is the chief surveyor of Colter Surveying Company, the company that was hired by the SFP&P to survey the route from Ash Fork to Prescott, including the disputed section of the line."

The judge narrowed his eyes at Sam. Certainly, he realized that family dynamics were at play. Then he waved Boone forward.

Boone explained the map of the land, the proposed route, and the geology.

"The geology and the line's trajectory from the north make this the only viable place to run the line," he said as he pointed to the spot on the map. "The SFP&P will have to blast rock to make the line work."

"Were there other alternatives to the east or the west?" Alex asked.

"This area drops steeply into a ravine, so a bridge is not an option. To the east, we could run the line here, but that would cut much deeper into the Colter Ranch property, severing a critical section of their grazing lands. We felt that the proposed route offered the best solution for both the SFP&P and Colter Ranch."

The judge nodded.

"No further questions for this witness," Alex stated.

Rankin declined to question Boone.

"We call James Colter, Vice President of Transportation for the SFP&P to the stand."

"Colter?" The judge frowned and sighed heavily. "Proceed."

I took the stand and swore to tell the truth.

"Mr. Colter, please state your responsibilities at the railway for the court."

I smiled. "Certainly. As the Vice President of Transportation, I oversee the construction, reviewing the survey reports, and handing off the reports to our construction engineers. I am also responsible for the schedules and general operations of the trains once they are in service."

"In your role, did you review the survey report presented by Boone Colter?"

"Yes. In fact, my instructions to him when he surveyed the route was to do his best to avoid splitting off large sections of the ranchers' lands, including several ranches near Ash Fork."

"So, you requested Boone Colter to find the most workable route with the least impact on any privately owned land?"

"That is correct."

"When the SFP&P presented the route to the Arizona Ter-ritorial Legislature, did the SFP&P present multiple options?"

"We presented the option that allowed the SFP&P the land needed to build the railway with the least impact to private owners. The members of the Legislature did question us about alternatives, and we presented them, but showed that our preference was to, again, choose the route that affected private owners the least."

"Thank you. No further questions or witnesses," Alex said.

The judge halted Rankin before he started speaking. "In my opinion, Mr. Rankin, this is a frivolous case. The SFP&P has worked with your client and other ranchers like him. If you ask me, this is a family dispute and not an overstepping of the railway. I'm throwing this case out."

Sam crossed his arms and glared at me as the judge allowed me to take a seat again.

The judge banged his gavel. As the sound reverberated, I prayed Sam and Papa would forgive me soon for taking the small corner of their land. Thankfully, the case proved I did my best to take as little of their land as possible.

As we left the courtroom, I thanked Alex and Keri for their work on getting the case thrown out. A minor part of me hoped that one day soon, I might pick up a relationship with her. She was in my thoughts more often.

CHAPTER 6

Prescott, Arizona Territory
April 24, 1893

JAMES

I took a deep breath as I stepped onto the train station platform and walked toward the beautiful black Engine No. 4. The Brooks 8-Wheel Locomotive pointed northeast on the tracks, ready for its first passenger trip. A deep sense of satisfaction settled over me as I ran a hand over the side of the engineer's cab. The engine sat atop four sixty-four-inch wheels near its back. Four smaller wheels supported the front of the magnificent machine just behind the v-shaped grate.

The same sense of exhilaration that I felt seeing my first engine filled me now as I watched the fireman toss coal into the firebox. The engineer started the iron beast. Soon after, a white cloud of steam billowed out of the engine's exhaust. When he caught sight of me, the engineer pulled the rope for the train whistle, which echoed through the train station.

As the ceremony started, I faded into the crowd and

watched as the last spike was driven into the ground in Prescott. The line between Ash Fork and Prescott opened at last. The air buzzed with anticipation, matching the same feeling rising in my chest.

My work towards that goal started over two and a half years prior when I first approached my brother Boone to conduct some of the earliest surveys. Eight million dollars later, the line that Frank and I dreamed about was finally a reality.

Only one person came to mind that I wanted to share the day with.

"Mr. Colter," a feminine voice called my name. My heart danced at her greeting.

I turned around to face Keri Glassman before I kissed her cheek as if we were old friends. My pulse picked up pace as I studied her appearance. Her light blue dress hugged her curves in a very pleasing, yet tasteful way. The color brought out the deep blue of her eyes, eyes that called to me years ago. I never forgot those eyes. A matching blue hat with ivory lace topped her long hair, which was fashioned into a knot at the base of her graceful neck.

"I see you received my invitation." I flashed her what I hoped was a charming smile.

She smiled, and those blue eyes sparkled. "I did. Papa was a little miffed the invitation did not include him and Mama."

"Frank and I agreed to only one invitation per executive."

As color dusted her cheeks, she reached up to touch her graceful neck. "Thank you for the extraordinary opportunity."

"It was the least I could do for the woman who saved us three hundred thousand dollars."

Keri took my arm as I helped her onto the train. When we took our seats, she continued. "I'm surprised you remember that."

"Two things I remember well. Sizeable sums of money and a beautiful woman."

"Oh? Have there been many beautiful women?" she asked.

"Just the one."

Her gaze darted to the floor. "Then I feel truly honored to be included in the inaugural trip."

A smile stretched across my lips as I remembered every encounter with her over the past few years, from the dance at our first celebration to the moment we watched the construction of the World's Fair in Chicago. I never contacted her because of her age. When I learned she turned eighteen a few weeks ago, I wanted to see if any of those old feelings still existed. Judging by my catapulting pulse, they did. With the completion of the line to Prescott, I hoped to start a social life, and I wanted it to include her.

"You look lovely, by the way."

"Thank you."

"I heard a rumor that congratulations are in order."

She quirked an eyebrow.

"You passed the bar."

Her pink lips formed a full smile. "Yes, just last week. My name joined the handful of other women attorneys in the territory, including my mother."

As the train pulled away from the station, I leaned forward to peer out the window. She watched as well. After a few minutes, we passed through Granite Dells.

"My goodness," she said. "Such a lovely area. It reminds me of the large rock formations near Grandpa's ranch."

She giggled. "I suppose it is your family's ranch as well.

Sometimes I forget that was your home growing up."

I snorted. "I think sometimes I forget, too. It's been a decade since I left."

"That long?" she asked.

As I tried not to think about what her age was when I left, I thought it might be foolish to think I could win her heart.

"Oh, I'm sorry. I didn't mean to…"

The silence stretched as I tried to say something clever. Words rarely failed me, but at that moment, none came to my aid.

"I'm sure today is a big milestone in your life," she said, deftly changing the subject. "You finally get to see your dreams and plans come to fruition."

I smiled. "Yes, it is."

"How long is the ride to Ash Fork?" she asked.

"A few hours."

As the train wound its way through the spectacular scenery, my joy increased. It was not like we strategically planned a scenic route. It just happened that way. What a fantastic marketing opportunity. I considered if we might add a shorter trip mid-way as a weekend picnic getaway for sweethearts. I'd certainly like to take advantage of such an opportunity.

"How long did it take to build?" she asked.

"We started construction out of Phoenix to Wickenburg in 1891 and finished it at the end of the year. The construction in Ash Fork started in January 1892. So, it was one year and four months."

"Didn't Bullock build his line faster? Six months I believe."

I frowned at the mention of my former employer's name. "He took shortcuts and used poor quality construction. That's why his line is closed for construction from time to time. We built our line to last."

"It must have taken a lot of manpower to build it."

"That and coordination. And, of course, money." And a few lives. One life was too many, but we lost a dozen.

"What's wrong?" she asked as she took my hand.

I schooled my expression. "Nothing."

Then I took a deep breath and smiled before I laced my fingers with hers.

Her raised eyebrow told me she didn't believe my procla-mation that it was nothing. But she did not press me on it.

"Are you going to keep working for your parents?"

"I'm not sure, but I have no other offers. Contract law is something I enjoy. I like details. Things jump off the page at me." She laughed. "My papa says it's a gift."

She looked out the window.

"Do what you were created to do," she muttered.

"What's that?"

"Oh," she smiled at me again. "It's something Grandpa used to always say that Papa picked up. He drilled it into our heads as children. 'Do what you were created to do. Be what God made you to be.'"

The words landed on my heart like a sledgehammer. I never asked what I was created to be. Instead, I saw an op-portunity, capitalized on it, grew whatever business I worked in, before I moved onto the next. I wondered if that was what I was created to do. It seemed to fit me. Doing anything else never crossed my mind.

"And what did God create Keri Glassman to be?"

"A contract lawyer. Among other things."

"Other things?"

"Yes."

I laughed. "Alright. I won't press."

When the train slowed and stopped, she looked around. "Why are we stopping?"

"The county inspector scheduled a few random stops today to inspect the line. We shouldn't be here long."

I stood.

"Would you care to stretch your legs?"

As she placed her hand on mine, lightning coursed up my arm. The desire to spend more time with her filled my soul. No longer would I allow months or years to separate us.

As the county's agent inspected the line, I led Keri to the back vestibule.

"What is he looking for?"

"Proper number of ties and spikes. Quality of the steel. Splits in the wooden ties. He won't find any issues."

"You sound very confident."

"We have our own inspectors that travel the line ahead of every train. We won't roll out of the station if the line isn't safe."

While she watched the inspector's every movement, I slid my arm around her. As she placed her arm around my waist, I nearly stopped breathing at her light touch. Once the inspector walked back toward the train, I released my hold and led Keri back to our seats.

For the rest of the train ride, I asked about her family, and she told me stories about her younger brothers and sisters. She was the oldest, like me. I couldn't decide if her desire to be a contract lawyer was ambitious or practical. In some ways, she reminded me of myself. Yet in other ways, she was so different from me.

The more time I spent with her, the more interested I grew.

CHAPTER 7

KERI

When I quoted my father, I nearly kicked myself. The natural question James asked after my declaration should not have surprised me.

"What did God create Keri Glassman to be?"

"A contract lawyer." A daughter, sister, wife, and mother.

Like my mother, I wanted it all. I wanted a career, a marriage as happy as hers, and children. I would not sacrifice a family for a career. Mama successfully navigated it all. I believed I could as well.

"Other things."

"Other things?"

I glanced at his fingers interlaced with mine. It felt so natural to touch him. To talk to him. But I didn't know him. We danced together on one magical night. I worked on a case for him. I read some contracts for him in Chicago and watched the construction of the World's Fair with him. That hardly qualified as a relationship worthy of revealing my soul. It seemed unwise to elaborate on the thoughts churning in my heart, despite his veiled confession earlier that I was the only woman to capture his attention. Even if he complimented me and told me I was beautiful. His words made my heart flutter when he first said them and again as I reflected on them.

"Yes." I finally answered his question. It was the only word I felt comfortable sharing at that moment.

As he let it go, I breathed a soft sigh of relief.

Once we arrived in Ash Fork, James took my things and handed them to the porter at the station. He paid to have them delivered to my room at the hotel.

Things like that confused me. Was he just being kind? Or I should expect him to do something like that for me? Papa always did little things for Mama. Grandpa did the same for Grandma. Yet, I observed many men who did nothing of the sort for their wives. I filed it away in my mind to ask Papa later.

As James guided me to the hotel for supper, I placed my hand in the crook of his arm. With every touch, I became more aware of him. My pulse raced. My arms tingled. Like the dance years ago, I wanted to be around him more and I had no desire to leave his company.

When we arrived in the dining room, he held out a chair for me before he sat opposite from me.

"Would you care for some wine?"

Even though Papa allowed me to have wine from time to time with supper and I liked it, I declined.

James smiled at me. "Iced tea then?"

I nodded, then I perused the menu. "Do you have a recommendation?"

He laughed nervously. "It's my first time dining here too."

"Really? You never ate here during the construction of the line?"

He shook his head. "No. I had a private suite in a railcar, which I rode to the construction site. We had a cook who provided meals for all the management and staff."

"Then I will try the duck. I can't recall a time when I've eaten duck."

"Feeling adventurous?"

"You seem to bring that out in me." I looked down as my cheeks warmed. I meant to keep that thought private.

"Then I will take the elk."

"Surely, you've eaten elk before. You grew up on a ranch. Why, I imagine you downed one yourself when you were young?"

He smiled. "I've eaten elk before. Just not in years. And yes, I did hunt when I lived on the ranch. A Colter not learning how to hunt is sacrilegious."

"Did you like it?"

"The elk or hunting?"

"Both I suppose." I leaned forward as he spoke. His brown eyes danced with amusement.

"I enjoyed hunting with Boone. Mostly because he did all the work. I enjoyed eating the elk that he brought home. Butchering the thing disturbed me."

"So, you don't hunt anymore?"

"Not if I can avoid it."

As the server delivered our meals, James took my hand and prayed over the meal. It caught me off guard. I did not picture him doing so. Yet the act seemed effortless and natural.

After he released my hand, I ate a piece of duck. It melted in my mouth. My eyes rounded in surprise.

"It's good?"

"Would you like to try a bite?" I offered as I cut a piece off and held it up for him.

He stared at it for a few seconds, then he opened his mouth and ate it from my fork. He nodded.

"That is good. Would you like to try the elk?"

"No, thank you. I've eaten elk many times. Grandpa or Uncle Adam often hunted for one at Christmas or family gatherings."

He frowned. "I guess I never realized that he is an uncle to both of us."

"Well, he is Mama's brother. And your Aunt Julia's husband." I smiled wryly.

"Yes. It was a silly thing to say."

I smiled. "Not so silly. Going to the ranch was a special treat for the Glassman family. It was your home. I don't suppose it stood out to you as being anything special."

"No. Ever since I turned fourteen, all my dreams were about the railroad. I only ever wanted to be a railroad man."

"And now you've built your own."

He smiled and straightened in his chair. "Yes, I did."

"It's a fine railroad. I'm delighted for you, James."

As his gaze connected with mine, I became lost in his dark brown eyes for several minutes. Something about him drew me in.

When my words came back to me, I said, "I know the people of Prescott will benefit from it. You've done a great thing."

"Thank you."

When I finished my duck, potatoes, and carrots, I pushed the plate back from the table.

"Care for some dessert?"

I shook my head and failed to stifle a yawn. "I guess I'm more tired than I thought."

"Let me walk you to your room."

After he paid for the meal, he escorted me to my room.

As he stood there, I looked up into his dark eyes. A strand of his brown hair drooped over his forehead. Surely, he felt the hum in the air when he stood so close to me that his breath warmed my face. He placed one hand on my waist. Then the other. The touch left me breathless.

"May I kiss you?"

I nodded.

Then he lowered his lips to mine. It was soft at first, sending thrilling shivers down my spine. So I leaned against him and placed my hands behind his neck. As he deepened the kiss, I kissed him back with feelings I never knew I had. When his hands roamed over my back, my heart longed for him. Slowly, his hands returned to my waist. Gently, his lips pulled away from mine and the blissful experience ended.

My hands remained clasped behind his neck as my breathing eased. He lifted a finger and trailed it along my cheek. Then he released his other hand from my waist before he took my hands and unclasped them from behind his neck. He took a step back, and I immediately missed his nearness. My eyes never left his as I smoothed out my skirt.

"Good night, Keri. Thank you for coming."

Unable to speak through the thick air, I smiled.

When he turned and walked down the hall, I turned toward my door and unlocked it. As I glanced over my shoulder, he looked over his. His smile sent tingles down my spine and heat warmed my middle before I ducked into my room and closed the door.

He kissed me. It was a wonderful kiss. Not that I had anything to compare it to. I was no longer a schoolgirl or a studious young attorney. Now I was a woman. A woman desired by a man.

I numbly sat on the edge of my bed and let my thoughts and feelings settle. I saw myself falling for James.

CHAPTER 8

JAMES

It was harder than I thought to let go of Keri after kissing her. She felt perfect in my arms, like she belonged right there. My feelings for her had grown stronger over the years, much to my surprise. I took a shaky breath as I opened the door to my room. I closed it before I leaned against it.

When I said only she captured my attention, I told the truth. Over the years, several prominent men tried to foist their daughters on me. Senators. Mayors. Businessmen. Some women were beautiful. Some would have made an excellent companion.

None compared to Keri Glassman. Though her beauty stole my attention, it was everything else about her that kept it. She was intelligent, quietly ambitious, observant, and far more mature than her age would lead one to believe.

As I untied my neck scarf and laid my jacket over the back of a chair in my suite, I walked to the window to study the town. Lights glowed in the saloon at the opposite end of the main street. A few pedestrians walked in front of the closed businesses.

I wasn't tired, so I sat in a plush chair and tried to read

by the lamplight. Except my mind failed to focus on the words on the page. That day, my dream of becoming a railroad owner came true. Ten years of hard work. Ten years working my way up through various lines. Patience. Diligence. Negotiating. Planning. Executing on those plans.

I thought I would be happier. I thought I would feel fulfilled. Complete.

Yet, I felt as empty as always. It bothered me. I wondered if that emptiness was loneliness. Was it the drive that propelled me forward to the next venture?

Perhaps Frank found satisfaction in our accomplishment, though I doubted it. We still needed to complete the line between Prescott and Wickenburg. Then we discussed several other opportunities. It seemed our ideas never dried up, and we never finished. There was always more to do.

After I rubbed a hand over my face, I changed out of my clothes and climbed into bed. As I stared up at the ceiling, restlessness creeped into my mind. I ought to be satisfied, but I wasn't. Something was wrong with me. I failed to celebrate accomplishments. I failed to live in the moment. When the future arrived, it seemed less than I expected. I rolled onto my side and closed my eyes as I begged for sleep to calm my mind.

In the middle of the night, I woke with a start. The smell of smoke hung heavily in the air. I jumped out of bed and dressed quickly. I looked out the window. The glow of fire lit the night sky.

I coughed on the smoke in my room.

Then my brain woke fully. The hotel was on fire!

I touched the door. No heat. I opened it. Others filed into the hallway.

"Go! Get out!" I yelled.

Men and women ran to the stairs.

Keri.

My heart sank. My lungs squeezed tight. She was on the next floor up. I ran against the surge of people.

"Keri!"

Nothing.

I made it into the hallway as flames licked the walls. I covered my mouth and nose with my handkerchief. My eyes stung. I strained to see her room, but I couldn't.

A man grabbed my arm and pulled me back into the stair-well.

"Keri!"

He pushed me forward downstairs with the throng of people.

Once I arrived in the open night air, I searched the faces of the crowd, and stuffed my handkerchief in my pocket.

"Keri!"

No answer.

Someone handed me a bucket of water. A water line formed around me, so I turned my attention to the fire. All the while, I tried to look for her.

The building next to the hotel caught fire. I handed the bucket to another man, and I walked deeper into the street. I turned around in a circle. The entire town blazed against the starry sky, including the train station.

The crisis manager in me sprang into action. I ran toward the train station's bunkhouse. It too was on fire, but my employees were safely out. I found the train engineer and crew.

"Get this train out of here!" I barked the order. "Start it down toward Chino Valley. Priority is water."

I knew the town relied on water transported up from Chino Valley. The survivors needed water and we must ship it in.

"Where's the telegrapher?"

He stepped forward.

"Can you tap into the line outside of town?"

"Yes, sir. It will take me a minute. And I could use someone who can scale the pole to cut the line and drop it down."

"I'll help," a strapping young man volunteered.

"Go. Wire down to Prescott that there's a fire in Ash Fork. The whole town is burning down. Ask them to send the train with supplies, food, clothing, water from Chino Valley, and whatever else they can send."

The two men ran down the line to send messages to the south.

I turned to the rest of the employees. "Were you able to salvage blankets or other supplies?"

A few people came forward at first. We started a pile of things that we collected. Then more people added to it. A pastor and his wife showed up to help. Then a doctor. Women volunteered to help the injured.

I glanced up at the telegraph lines. The A&P line was still intact and would enable us to send messages to the east and west. I darted into the burning station and rescued the telegraph machine. Another worker helped tap into the A&P line. I tried to remember Morse code. It had been years since I used it.

I tapped out that the message was an open message to all stations. "Ash Fork burned to ground. Send lumber. Send men. Doctors."

The line clicked. I tried to decipher the message as it came across. I only caught a few words. It was enough. Lumber was on its way from Flagstaff. Williams was sending men and supplies by train. Seligman was sending a water car.

The telegrapher found me and reported in. "Prescott and Chino Valley are sending food, water, clothes, blankets, and people to help."

"Excellent. By morning, we should be able to take care of everyone and start rebuilding."

As I took a deep breath, the faces in the crowd stared at me. Hope flickered in their eyes. They would get through the night.

The station manager joined me to help with planning.

"We need to store the lumber away from any lingering embers. Preferably on the east side of town since the lumber will come from Flagstaff."

A group of men volunteered to unload the lumber.

As others or I came up with specific ideas to help, I gathered the volunteers and assigned them their duties.

The glow of burning buildings dimmed just before dawn. As the sun rose, I surveyed the damage. Only a handful of buildings remained. The fire swept through the town like a tinderbox and swallowed most every structure.

Horses plodded down the street. Several men rounded them toward a makeshift corral. Men, women, and children huddled together with their soot-stained faces.

The last time I had the misfortune of leading after a crisis, I failed to give the people hope. Ironically, my mother took the lead that time.

"Listen up!" I shouted. "Gather around!"

People pushed closer to the train station platform. I stood as high as I could so my voice would carry.

"Supplies are on the way. Food. Water. Medical help. Materials to rebuild."

The people murmured. I motioned my hands downward to quiet them down.

"We need to help each other. Search the rubble for survivors if you can. Help treat the wounded, if you can. If you're weary, then rest. We will help each other. The railways will help."

I felt confident the A&P would help, even though I had no authority to speak on their behalf.

"Help is on the way. We will get folks back to their homes as soon as possible. In the meantime, if you see a need, please take care of it."

The crowd dispersed. I scanned their faces for Keri. She was nowhere to be found.

Lord, please let her be safe.

CHAPTER 9

KERI

My pleasant dreams quickly turned to nightmares, which caused me to bolt upright in bed. I gasped for air. Smoke coated my lungs and burned my eyes.

I dropped to the floor below the thickest of the smoke. I heard screams from the hallway. No time to retrieve my things. I sensed the danger. I must go now.

I crawled toward the door. Then I reached up and opened it. Fire devoured the wallpaper. I crouched and headed toward the closest stairwell as I gathered my night-gown up so my bare feet did not trip over the hem.

Creaking wood sounded above me. I ran.

A crash echoed. Air pushed me forward into the wall of the stairwell. My head hit a sharp corner. Moisture trickled down the side of my face.

Someone hauled me to my feet and dragged me forward. My head pounded. I coughed. I scampered down the stairs. The rough wood sliced at my feet. I hurried, ignoring the pain and the screams filling the night air.

At last! Fresh air. Starry sky.

I stumbled forward before I collapsed to the ground in a

heap.

James.

I glanced around but didn't see him.

My vision blurred. My head swam. I touched the warm liquid on the side of my face. I looked at my fingers and the sticky substance that coated them. Blood.

Coughs shook my body. Air failed to fill my lungs.

I went limp as my face landed in the dirt. My eyes closed.

"Miss. Miss!"

Someone shook my body. I groaned.

"Wake up."

I opened my eyes as the sun splayed glorious colors across the sky. I sat up.

"What?" I moaned at the pain everywhere.

"Can you stand?" A young saloon girl asked me.

"I…"

"Here, put your arm around my shoulders."

I did as she said.

"What's your name?" she asked.

"Keri. Glassman."

"Nice to meet you, Keri. I'm Sapphire."

I snorted.

"I see you're well enough to know that's not my real name."

She looped an arm around my waist. Then we stood together.

"Let's go to the doctor."

The pounding in my head made the walk nearly unbearable. It felt like we walked for miles.

An older woman helped me sit on the ground.

"This here's Keri. Found her over by the hotel."

"Thank you, Sapphire," the older woman said.

"Keri, my name is Iris. I'm the pastor's wife."

I nodded. Then I groaned and closed my eyes.

"Where does it hurt?"

"My head."

A cool cloth blotted the sticky blood from the side of my face.

"You've got a nice sized knot there. And a gash. Anything else hurt?"

"I don't think so."

"Looks like your feet are pretty cut up too."

I waved her hands away from my feet.

"Here," I said. "I can wash my face."

She handed me the cloth.

"Take care of someone else worse off."

She smiled. "Alright. I think you're spunky enough to manage for now. Don't get up quickly. And try to stay awake. That bump concerns me."

As she turned away, I grabbed her arm. "Have you found a man named James?"

"No. Is he your husband?"

"A friend."

She nodded. "I'll send him over if he shows up."

"Thank you."

Iris left.

Once I finished wiping off my face, I looked around slowly. Fast movements made my head hurt. Thirty people sat or lied around me in a triage area. Most were in night clothes like me. Several looked badly burned.

Lord, please help these people.

In the distance, I could see a crowd gathering by the train station. They quieted. A man spoke to them, but I was too far away to hear. As the crowd dispersed, more people gathered around the injured.

"What did he say?" I asked a young woman.

"Help is on the way. Food, water, blankets, medical help. He even said lumber was coming from Flagstaff. Can you believe it?"

"Who was he?"

"He looked like a fancy businessman. I think someone said he works with the new railroad."

James. Could it be?

I tried to stand, but she suggested I stay put, as I didn't look good.

The pounding in my head continued. I laid down on my side and slept.

"Keri!"

My name. I slowly sat up.

"Keri!"

The second time sounded far away.

"Over here!" I waved my arm as I propped my head on my other hand.

"Keri!" The voice came closer.

"Oh, thank God!"

James dropped to his knees and gathered me in his arms. He kissed my forehead. Then he held me away from him.

"You're hurt."

I smirked. "A little."

"Are you being sassy?"

"A little."

He draped his jacket over my shoulders. Then he put one arm in the sleeve. Then the next.

He dipped my head and inhaled a sharp breath. "That's a nasty bump and cut."

"So, Iris said."

He moved to sit next to me and placed his arm around me. "I was worried you didn't…" His voice caught. "Make it out."

His fingers rubbed my arm.

"I'm tired."

"Lean up against me. Close your eyes."

As his arms wrapped around me to shelter me from the chaos, I rested against him and fell asleep.

———

Sometime later, I woke near the train platform as I heard voices around me.

"The lumber arrived from Flagstaff."

"Thank you. Ralph, was it?"

"Yes sir, Mr. Colter."

"Water is almost here," another man said.

"Excellent, Horace."

"James." I said his name as I sat up. "What's going on?"

He kneeled next to me. "I hope it's alright I moved you. I wanted to check on you while I coordinated the relief efforts."

"Can I help?"

He smiled and brushed his fingers along my cheek. "Just knowing you're safe is enough for now. I promise I'll get you home as soon as I can."

As the fog in my brain cleared later in the day, I took part in the relief efforts, much to James's dismay. The Santa Fe, Prescott, & Phoenix arrived at the station. When employees dumped supplies along the platform, I organized the supplies by type. I sent the medical supplies over to the doctors as soon as possible. Then I asked volunteers to group the food together. If something was ready to consume, I asked for folks to distribute it immediately.

James found me late in the day. "Have you eaten anything?"

"No. You?"

"Not yet. We should get some water and food."

He led me over to where volunteers distributed food and water. We waited in the long line.

"Your feet." He gasped. "Do you want my shoes?"

I laughed as I held my dainty foot next to his long foot. "I don't think it would be helpful."

"We'll get you some shoes. I think I saw a crate of them come in."

We stepped forward in the line.

"I think there were some clothes, too."

I held his jacket closer. "I kinda like this."

"Alright. I'm getting the feeling you might be stubborn."

"I prefer to call it persistent. I am my father's daughter."

He grinned.

Once we got to the front of the line, he carried my food and water along with his. Then we wandered to the train station platform and sat down to eat.

"Some first date," he muttered.

"Oh, was this a date?"

"Well, the train ride was. The fire, eh, that was an unplan-ned light show."

I ate a bite of my sandwich.

"I promise the next one won't be as eventful."

"You're assuming I will say yes to the next one." I school-ed my features.

He studied me for a moment.

I couldn't keep from smiling.

"I thought so," he said. "You had me there for a minute."

"I think it will be hard to top this date. I mean burning down a town..."

He laughed. "Your humor is a little unladylike, don't you think?"

"Like I said, I'm my father's daughter. If we can't laugh in the face of tragedy, then what hope is there?"

"True."

As night fell around the town, the activity quieted. People found places to sleep. James's employees handed out blankets to as many people as they could. Thankfully, James gave me his blanket before I found a spot with the women who worked for the railroad.

CHAPTER 10

JAMES

Two days after the fire, the town began rebuilding. The passengers from the inaugural trip on the SFP&P boarded the train for home. I rode next to an exhausted Keri. At least we found a dress and some shoes for her. I watched her as she slept on the train ride back to Prescott.

Whatever first drew me to her grew deep roots in my heart over the past two days. She handled a crisis with dignity and laughter. She helped many people regardless of their station in life. I admired her character.

When she woke, I posed a question to her. "Will you work for the SFP&P?"

"Doing what?"

"As our contract attorney," I said. I hoped she would say yes. Even if she didn't, I planned to pursue a courtship with her.

She thought for a moment. "Don't you already have someone reviewing your contracts?"

I hesitated. "We have general counsel, but he is overworked. He doesn't have the time to give contracts a proper review. Not like you do."

"Would that be my only responsibility? Are there that many contracts?"

"There are a lot of contracts. Running a railway involves more than what people think. If that doesn't keep you busy enough, you could help the general counsel."

"Who would I report to?"

I thought for a moment. I never discussed such a position with Frank. He might be upset about it.

"Me."

"Alright. But I expect a fair salary. I'm a fully licensed attorney that has apprenticed with two licensed attorneys for several years. I expect to be compensated at a salary commen-surable with a male counterpart."

I smiled. "You'll make a great contract attorney. All those words to say you want a fair wage. Done."

"When do I start?"

"Monday?"

"Excellent."

I smiled and rested my arm across her shoulders.

We spent the rest of the trip in silence. When we arrived in Prescott, I helped her down from the train.

"Keri!"

I recognized her father's voice.

"I'll see you Monday," she said before she greeted her father.

"What happened? Your face. Your clothes."

I lingered for a minute.

"I'll tell you about it on the way home," she said. Then she turned to me. "I'll see you soon."

Then she walked away with her father.

I sighed. Monday could not come soon enough.

In the meantime, I went home, cleaned up, and headed into the office to do some damage control.

———

"You did what?" Frank asked as he drummed his fingers on the top of his large cherry wood desk when I delivered the news on Friday morning.

As I closed his office door, I reiterated what I said a moment ago. "I hired a contract attorney."

"Is it Miss Glassman?"

I nodded.

"You hired your sweetheart for a job that did not exist and without consulting me." Frank shook his head. "Love and work don't mix, James."

"She's not my sweetheart." Yet.

Frank snorted. "Everyone who was on that train would disagree with you."

"She saved us three hundred thousand dollars."

"A year ago. What makes you think we need a contract attorney?"

I straightened in the chair. "Do you know how many contracts arrive in one week?"

"A dozen?"

"Twenty-five or more. A week."

Frank leaned back as he rubbed a hand on his chin.

"Who is reviewing those now?"

Frank cleared his throat.

"No one. Also, no one is auditing the invoices we receive to make sure the payments requested match up to the contract. No one in accounting knows the terms, much less if a vendor is overcharging us."

Frank narrowed his eyes at me.

"We could lose thousands we are not contractually obligated to pay."

"Fine. Give her a three-month trial basis. If she doesn't

save us more money than her salary, we cut her loose."

I was not happy with Frank's terms, as my theory about us overpaying was only a gut instinct at that point. I had no evidence to back it up.

"If you aren't satisfied in three months, then I will pay her out of my salary."

Frank launched to his feet and extended his hand. "You're a fool, but I'll take those terms."

I shook his hand.

"Love and work, James. You'll see what I mean."

I turned and left his office. He might be right. I might be a fool. Or I might just be a genius.

As I walked past my secretary's desk, I asked him to join me in my office.

"Morning, Gerard. How are you today?"

"Fine, sir." He took a seat across from my desk as I sat down.

"First order of business: send a memo to the superin-tend-ent of traffic to schedule a day trip on the weekends. Once you hear from him, have marketing advertise for a 'Picnic with your sweetheart'. Make sure it's a lovely place to stop. Have the superintendent stop the train for an hour while couples enjoy their picnic."

"Yes, sir."

"We have a new contract attorney starting on Monday, so I'll need you to find an office for her."

Gerard raised an eyebrow. "Her? An office and not a desk?"

"An office. She will work with sensitive documents."

"Yes, sir." He ran a finger along his neckline. I knew he would make it happen, even if it made him uncomfortable.

"Miss Glassman will also need access to a person in ac-counting to audit invoices per her instructions based on what she reviews in the contracts."

Gerard scribbled down a note while I continued. "She also has full authority to renegotiate contracts with me as the final approver. If she asks for your help, you will give it."

Gerard frowned that time. "Sir?"

"Was I unclear?"

He cleared his throat. "No, sir."

"When she arrives on Monday morning, I'll meet with her and show her to her office, so clear my morning. She will report directly to me."

When I motioned for him to leave, he stood and walked out of the office stiffly. I knew bringing a woman into the office would ruffle some feathers, especially with the level of responsibility and autonomy I planned to give Keri. The male staff would be upset I gave her an office, but one didn't get to my position without knowing how to navigate those things.

Besides, she was not the only woman in the office. We had several typists, a cook, and a handful of secretaries that were women. It was the way of the future.

By midafternoon, the superintendent of traffic, Daniel Parker, asked me to stop by. I entered his office.

"Mr. Colter, here's what we've come up with for the weekend excursion." He rounded his desk and pointed out the route on the map. "We'll stop at Rock Butte, where the passengers can see the trestles. There's a delightful spot here," he pointed to it on the map, "for a picnic. We can charge $3.60 round trip."

"You're married, right?"

He nodded.

"Why don't you test it out this Sunday afternoon with your wife? Offer the trip to other married employees, then let's solicit their feedback on Monday."

Daniel grinned. "That would be wonderful. Thank you, Mr. Colter."

Within the hour, he arranged everything and sent out an interoffice memo. Gerard brought it to me. I read over the details and smiled. It was a great idea.

As evening settled over the town, I left the office. I started toward home, then I turned around. Even though it was impulsive, I wanted to see Keri, so I strolled toward the Glassman home and hoped that I would be welcome.

CHAPTER 11

KERI

"We received the message that there was a fire in Ash Fork," Papa said as he hugged me on the train station platform.

After I said my farewells to James, I turned to my papa. "Yes, it happened overnight."

His eyes scanned my face and stopped for a moment on the scratch over my right eye. He frowned. "Does it hurt?"

"Not really."

"Your mother is going to be upset. It looks pretty bad. Might turn into a scar."

I smiled. "Then it will add a little character to my face."

Papa laughed. "Don't say that to your mother. She won't find it funny."

I looped my arm in his. "I suppose she won't like my new dress either."

"We can donate it."

We walked a few blocks in silence before Papa spoke again. "I'm glad you're safe." He coughed. "I... I couldn't bear it if anything happened to my little girl."

"Papa, I'm not so little anymore. I can take care of myself."

He sniffed. "I know."

"Before the fire, I really enjoyed myself. James took me to dinner after the train ride." My voice held a dreamy quality.

Papa sighed. "You like him, don't you?"

"Very much."

"I don't know if I'm ready for that, yet."

I hesitated and chose my next words carefully. "He offered me a job as a contract attorney."

Papa stopped and turned toward me. "Is he going to pay you a fair wage?"

"Of course. I'm going to be his contract attorney, so I proved my worth by negotiating, as I phrased it, 'a salary commensurate to a male colleague' or something like that."

Papa smiled and started walking again. "That's my girl."

"I start on Monday. I know it's not much notice."

"We talked about this kind of opportunity. You were wise to seize it. We'll manage."

"I'll help tomorrow."

"Thank you, Keri. I'm very proud of you."

I smiled as his praise settled over my heart.

"Is it too much to hope Mama will be as happy?"

He laughed. "You might leave out the part about being sweet on James Colter. She's definitely not ready for you to court."

I frowned as we stepped onto the sweeping porch of our home. Papa held the door open for me. As soon as I walked through the doorway, Mama ran to me and hugged me.

"Thank goodness you are alright. Let me look at you."

The moment she saw the gash on my forehead, a shadow settled over her countenance. Her eyes flashed with fear before concern replaced it.

"Are you alright?" she asked.

"I'm fine, Mama."

She examined me from head to toe. When she finished, she hugged me again.

Just then, our cook announced supper was ready, so we all headed into the dining room. As soon as Papa finished saying grace, my siblings peppered me with questions.

"Were you scared?" thirteen-year-old Archie asked.

"When I woke up to the smoke, yes. Once I made it out-side, I was fine."

"What was the train like?" nine-year-old Amelia asked.

"Did James kiss you?" sixteen-year-old Sadie asked.

My face heated at her question. Mama noticed.

"Did he?" she asked.

I raised my chin. "The train ride was enjoyable. The scenery is beautiful. We skirted the edge of Grandpa's ranch."

"You did?" eleven-year-old Clinton asked.

"Yes. I couldn't see any of the buildings, but I recognized the granite rock formations."

"Did James Colter kiss you?" Mama repeated her earlier question.

"What if he did?"

Mama frowned. "He's twenty-seven or twenty-eight."

"Mel." Papa's voice held a warning.

Mama pinned me down with her blue eyes. "We will talk about this later."

I took a bite of my food and gave one sharp nod. I didn't understand why Mama was being so difficult.

As soon as supper finished, Mama dragged me and Papa into Papa's den across from the dining room. Papa poured himself a whiskey. For once, I wished he might offer me a snifter. When he sat behind his desk, Mama angled her chair so she could see him and me. As Mama launched into her tirade, Papa took a sip.

"He's ten years older than you, which is far too old."

Papa raised an eyebrow in my direction.

"Did he kiss you?"

"Mama, they only allowed one invitation per executive for the train ride, and he asked me to go. I did. We enjoyed each other's company and conversation. He took me to dinner. He treated me with respect and dignity. After the fire, he found me and kept me safe. I helped him with the relief efforts. Anything else about the trip is none of your business."

Papa hid his smile behind his whiskey glass.

Mama sputtered, something I'd not witnessed before then. "None of my business! I'm your mother. It's my job to protect you."

On purpose, I sighed dramatically. "I'm not a child anymore. I'm an adult. My new job starts on Monday. I can decide on my own."

Mama frowned. "Alex, say something."

Papa took his sweet time sipping his whiskey. When Mama shot him daggers with her eyes, he set the glass down. He leaned forward on his elbows and tented his fingers.

"Mel, I must side with Keri on this one."

My eyes went wide, and I almost feared for his safety. Certainly, he could see Mama was livid with me.

He continued, "She is eighteen. She is ten years younger than James, yes. But you are nine years younger than me."

"That's different. When we met, I was much older."

"It really isn't different. Keri is a mature young woman of good moral character. She makes wise decisions. We've done our job to raise her well."

"And you raised me well," I interjected.

"Now, it's time for us to let her live the next stage of her life, to grow into independence. If she finds love along the way, so be it."

Mama sighed. "Now you sound like Papa."

Papa grinned. "Higher praise I've never heard."

I knew my papa admired and respected Grandpa and that he emulated Grandpa's romantic tendencies, even though he was Grandpa's son-in-law.

Mama stood and started toward the door.

"Mel." Papa's tone stopped her. "Let Keri go while you and I talk. The last few days have taken a toll on her."

Mama raised her chin and took a seat again. Papa nodded and excused me. I stood and closed the door behind me.

Being the oldest sometimes held its disadvantages. I was the first to walk into womanhood, and it scared my mother. I was the first to force my independence. That always caused friction between me and my mother. Papa understood it all. He often acted as peacemaker between us, though I rarely held a grudge and often sought peace with Mama.

I climbed the stairs and headed to the washroom. I drew a steamy bath, grateful for the luxury of indoor plumbing. While the water filled the tub, I grabbed my nightgown from my bedroom. Then I returned to wash my hair and bathe.

When I finished, I put on my nightgown and robe. Then I went downstairs to the parlor. I sat by the fire in the fireplace to dry my hair. Papa joined me.

"Give her time. She just needs to warm up to the idea that you're an adult."

I snorted. "I've worked with you at the law office for years now. What more do I have to do?"

"It's not about you at all. It's about her learning to let go of her children."

"And," I rolled my eyes, "I'm the first."

"Precisely."

———

Friday evening, around the time I thought Mama warmed up to the idea of me seeing James, I heard a commotion in the parlor. I hurried downstairs and stopped halfway when I saw James standing in the doorway.

My heart beat a little faster. I touched my hair and hoped it looked fine. I straightened my back and smiled as I gracefully descended the remaining stairs.

Unfortunately, Mama was the one who answered the door and not Papa. Papa came in from his den.

"James," he greeted as he carefully stepped around Mama. "Come in."

James turned his bowler hat around in his hand as he balanced his walking stick in the crook of his arm. He looked ready to run until Papa offered his hand for a shake. James glanced at Mama. She glared at him.

I sighed and stepped forward.

"Good evening, James," I said.

When he saw me, his features softened. "Would you like to take a walk?"

As Mama objected, Papa took her arm and led her away from the entryway. He nodded to me.

"I would love to." As James put his hat back on, I rested my hand in the crook of his arm. Then I closed the door behind us.

He blew out a loud breath and led me down the porch stairs.

"I'm sorry," I said. "Mama can be overprotective."

He laughed nervously. "I originally came to invite you for a train ride and picnic on Sunday after church, but after your mother's reaction, I thought a walk might be the better way to ask you."

"Papa is on our side, so he'll help Mama be nicer next time."

He let out a long breath. "Would you?"

"Pardon?"

"Would you take a train ride and picnic with me? I promise, no fires, no unexpected dangerous surprises. Just a train ride for us and a bunch of other employees and a picnic lunch."

"Well, when you put it like that, it doesn't sound nearly as adventurous." I kept my gaze focused in front of us and my face stoic. When I felt his eyes on me, I smiled.

"Remind me never to play poker with you."

As I laughed, I said, "I would be terrible. I always give away my bluff."

He laughed. "So, is that a 'yes'?"

I glanced at him and lowered my eyes. Then I raised them to meet his gaze. "Yes."

"Shall I sit with you in church?" he asked.

"If you'd like."

He turned us back toward my house. "I wish I could walk with you longer, but I must be on my way."

He stopped at the bottom of the porch. My stomach fluttered when he leaned forward and placed a kiss on my cheek.

"See you on Sunday."

"Good night, James."

He smiled and disappeared down the street and into the night.

CHAPTER 12

JAMES

When I woke Sunday morning, I felt unusually nervous. Rarely, if ever, I felt nervous. I tossed my black neck scarf aside in favor of a light blue one. After I slicked my hair to the side, I donned my gray bowler hat, which matched my light gray suit.

Then I strode toward church on time for once. There would be no hiding from my family that day. It would be impossible to sit next to Keri in secret.

A part of me regretted asking to sit next to her in church. Most people would see it for what it was, a public declaration of my interest in her. The only problem with such a public act was that my family, especially Mama, would be completely shocked. I never showed up to church on time, much less with a woman.

I cleared my throat as I approached the church.

"James!"

I closed my eyes at the sound of Mama's voice. After a second, I opened them and strode toward her as I pasted a smile on my face.

"Mama." I leaned down and kissed her on the cheek.

"I haven't seen you at church in ages."

Mama didn't know I attended every week unless I traveled out of town. I showed up late and left before the end of the last song to avoid a confrontation with Sam.

Papa hugged me. Boone and Jaclyn heard the commotion and greeted me. Then Deacon, Grady, and Vi joined us.

Sam nodded from a distance. I figured he wouldn't greet me. He was still mad about the railroad cutting across one small corner of his land. His wife waved to me.

"Will you join us for supper at the ranch?" Mama asked.

"I'm sorry to disappoint you, Mama, but I have plans today."

"Oh." Her shoulders sagged, and I felt guilty.

"It's been such a long time since you've been out."

"When you're in town next, let's have lunch together."

She patted my cheek and smiled, but I saw the hurt in her eyes.

"If you'll excuse me," I said when I saw Keri.

She wore a lovely light pink silk gown edged in white lace. The low neckline stole my attention for a moment. My mouth went dry.

I waited for a few seconds so Mama wouldn't feel like I brushed her off. Then I strode toward Keri and her family. I held back a sigh as her mother glared at me.

When Keri noticed me, I smiled, and I greeted her with a kiss on the cheek. Partly because I wanted to and partly because it would irritate Mel.

"Morning, Keri."

"Good morning, James."

Alex greeted me. I said hi to each of Keri's siblings before I escorted her into church. Then we sat in the pew in front of her parents.

When I glanced over toward my family across the aisle, Mama smiled. I breathed a sigh of relief. At least one of our mamas was happy.

The surrounding whispers settled down when the music started. I sang quietly and held the hymnal for Keri. I listened to the sermon and considered the pastor's words, though nothing stuck out in my mind after the service.

As soon as the service was over, I escorted Keri outside without stopping to talk to either her family or mine. The train left a few minutes after we arrived.

She sighed. "The route really is beautiful. Are all these people employees?"

"And their wives. We're testing out the idea of a picnic excursion on the weekends."

I held her hand in mine and laced my fingers with hers. When she smiled, her beautiful sapphire eyes sparkled.

"Is there a reason your mother dislikes me?" I asked and immediately regretted it as her smile faded.

"She thinks you're too old for me, even though she forgets Papa is nine years older than her. I'm the oldest, so I pave the way for my siblings."

After a few moments of silence, she spoke.

"James, what do you do with your free time?"

I laughed. "What is free time? I work long hours and travel often. By the time my day ends, I fall into bed."

"So, you don't read or play the piano or cards?" She wink-ed at me.

"I read several newspapers, including the morning and evening edition of the Gazette. I read the papers from Chicago, even though the news is a few days old."

"But nothing for fun? Novels?"

I blinked. "Work is fun for me."

"I guess that explains why you haven't married yet." She

looked away.

"I haven't married because I have found no one I like well enough. Yet." I didn't want to admit there was some truth in her assessment.

"If you married, would you work less?"

"I don't know." I truly didn't know. If I came home to her, I might not want to work so late.

When the train stopped, the conductors handed out picnic baskets and blankets to each couple. As Keri held onto my arm, I carried them and led us to a shaded area with a magnificent view of Rock Butte. Then I shook out the blanket and set the basket down. After I helped Keri sit, I reclined on the blanket. I propped myself up on one arm.

Her eyes sparkled again, and my heart warmed. She leaned forward to look into the basket.

"What do we have? Looks like two sandwiches." She handed me one. "Some fruit and lukewarm tea."

"What kind of fruit?"

"Grapes."

"Shall I feed them to you?"

Her cheeks flushed pink. "I'm certain I can manage a few grapes."

"But wouldn't it be more fun?"

I winked at her. She sat up straighter and took a bite of her sandwich. I smiled and watched her eat.

"Aren't you hungry?"

I shrugged. "I was hoping to feed some grapes to my sweetheart."

She quirked an eyebrow. "Sweetheart?"

"I'd like you to be."

"I suppose I wouldn't mind being your sweetheart."

I laughed and grabbed the grapes. I plucked one off and popped it in my mouth.

"Do you ever give a straight answer?" I asked.

"I'm an attorney."

"See, there you go again."

When she took the grapes from my hand, she scooted closer. Then she held one between two fingers. I leaned forward and opened my mouth before she dropped it in.

She giggled. "You're right. It is kinda fun to feed my sweetheart grapes."

Then she plucked off another one and offered it to me. I held her hand steady and purposely let my lips linger over the tips of her fingers before I took the grape. The air cracked between us. She held her breath for a few seconds as she bit her lower lip.

I tugged on her hand to coax her to recline next to me. When she did, I took the grapes and held one for her. She slowly took the grape from my fingers with her lips as she lowered her gaze. When she revealed her sapphire pools, I nearly stopped breathing altogether. I doubted she fully understood how enticing that look was.

My fingers found their way to her graceful, silky neck. I pulled her toward me, and my lips crashed onto hers with a ferocity I had not intended. She pressed closer, and I lowered her to the ground as I kissed her sweet lips. When she moaned, I slowed the kiss. Then she placed her hand on the back of my neck and kissed me more fervently. I trailed my fingers along the side of her neck, down her arm and to her waist as I moved the basket aside. I pressed her body against mine. Her fingers brushed my hairline at the nape of my neck. Desire and longing overwhelmed my senses.

Suddenly, I halted the kiss and sat up, breathing hard before I embarrassed either of us. She smiled and slowly sat up.

I chugged some iced tea. Then I bit into my sandwich to distract me from the thoughts running through my mind.

Thoughts which surprised me. It was only our second date. Perhaps what we went through in Ash Fork brought us closer together faster than I expected.

When her breathing settled, I couldn't resist teasing her. "Didn't I tell you that feeding my sweetheart grapes would be fun?"

I chewed another bite of my sandwich as I watched her cheeks turn rosier. She said nothing while she finished her sandwich.

The train whistle blew. Smart, I thought. I'd tell Daniel it was a good idea to warn the passengers to pack up and board the train.

I gathered up the food we didn't eat into the basket. Then I stood and held out my hands to help Keri up. Though tempted to pull her close for another kiss, I decided against it. Instead, I kneeled, picked up the blanket, and shook it out. She took it from my hands and folded it neatly.

"Shall we?" I offered Keri my arm as I realized I missed observing the scenic area of the train stop. I would bring Keri back again, but I doubted I would see much more scenery than I had that day.

CHAPTER 13

KERI

James's kisses woke something in me that was both powerful and frightening. I longed to remain next to him on that picnic blanket all afternoon. While I panted, I slowly sat up and said nothing. I studied him as I finished my sandwich. His brown eyes clouded as he teased me. He tried to hide his desire, but I saw it in his eyes and heard it in his voice.

I took a drink of the tea before he stood and packed everything. Once I was on my feet again, I glanced around at the scenic spot. It was quite beautiful, and I was only a little sorry I missed noticing it.

Then he helped me back to the train.

"Excellent job, Henry," he said to the conductor before he guided me down the aisle to our seats.

"Do you know everyone's name?" I asked.

James chuckled. "No. I read his name tag. I try to use my employees' names when they wear one or when I remember their name. It makes them feel like what they do is important."

As he sat next to me, he laced his fingers with mine

again.

"And the work they do is important. It takes every person doing their best to make a railway run smoothly and provide a memorable experience to our passengers and customers."

I smiled. I liked he acknowledged workers regardless of their position in the company.

"Are you getting excited about your new job?" he asked.

"I'm a little nervous. Especially if these passengers work in the office. I want respect for the work I do and not the company I keep." I lowered my gaze, then slowly lifted it. "Even if the company I keep is so exemplary."

A hearty laugh escaped his lips. "That's unexpected. I thought you might say funny or handsome, not exemplary."

I beamed.

When we arrived back in Prescott, he set a leisurely pace back to my home. As he led me up the stairs of the porch, I was not ready for our date to end.

I turned to face him. "I had a wonderful time."

He placed his hands on my waist. "Me, too."

Whispered voices came from the other side of the door. We glanced at the window and saw the faces of my siblings press-ed against the glass.

He placed a chaste kiss on my cheek. "I'd like to give you a better kiss, but I'm afraid your brothers and sisters will say something to your mother. Don't want to give her more reason to hate me."

I frowned. "She doesn't hate you, James. She just doesn't know how to deal with me having a sweetheart."

His hands fell to his side. "I hope you are right."

As he stepped back, he said, "I look forward to working with you tomorrow." Then he dashed down the porch stairs and walked out of sight.

I opened the door.

"Good afternoon," I greeted my family.

"Did he kiss you?" Sadie asked.

My cheeks warmed and answered for me. I wanted to gag her, and I wished she would stop asking, especially in front of my parents.

"If you don't mind, I'd like to read in my room."

I grabbed my book from the end table and hurried upstairs before anyone else asked embarrassing questions about my date.

CHAPTER 14

KERI

The next morning, I rose and looked over my dresses. My father was an impeccable dresser, and I shared the same trait. I flipped through my selection of dresses and pulled out three different ones with a modest, high neckline. All silk. I stood back and considered the plum dress before I laid it down and picked up the brown dress the same color as James's eyes. When I held it up to my figure, I smoothed out the wrinkles. Then I set it aside and picked up the gray dress, which I quickly discarded and went back to the brown.

I sighed. Choosing a dress had never been difficult. My goal was to look smart and sophisticated without looking flashy.

In the end, I returned the plum and gray dresses to my closet and settled on the brown dress. I brushed out my hair and twisted it into a knot at the base of my neck. After I pinned an ivory cameo at the collar, I put on delicate pearl drop earrings. Then I grabbed my satchel and headed downstairs for breakfast.

When I entered the dining room, Papa smiled and

greeted me. "You look lovely and confident this morning."

I felt far from it, but I smiled and thanked him as I took my usual seat.

"Conservative," Mama said. "An excellent choice for an office full of men."

I rolled my eyes toward Sadie. She took a gulp of water to hide her smile.

When breakfast finished, I walked with my parents, like every other morning. Once I reached the street that led toward the SFP&P office, I said my farewells.

Papa kissed me on the cheek. "You'll do great."

Mama smiled and kissed my cheek without a word.

When I arrived at the SFP&P office, I entered the large brick building. I went to the front desk and gave my name. Then I waited for someone to escort me to my desk.

"Keri!" James hurried down the elegant staircase to my right. His smile warmed me, and his eyes sparkled.

I smiled softly. I did not expect him to show me around.

"Morning, Mr. Colter."

He waved his hand in the air. "Call me James."

At his lack of formality, I bristled. I would see how others addressed him and would correct him if he was only informal with me.

I followed him up the grand staircase to the second floor. He showed me down a hallway, which opened to a large area with dozens of desks in rows.

"This is where the typists work. If you need anything typed, give it to the supervisor. He prioritizes the work for the typists."

Then he led me to what could only be the executive suite. The brass lights mounted onto the wall cast a glow on the reflective gilded wallpaper. Wood wainscoting ran along the entire hall.

"This is Gerard, my secretary. Gerard, this is Miss Keri Glassman. If you need anything, Keri, Gerard will help you."

I extended my hand for a shake. Gerard shook it lightly as he glowered at me.

"This is my office here and Frank's is next to it. Yours is across from mine."

As he held the door open, I stepped into the office, which was larger than my bedroom at home. An ornately carved wood desk stood facing two chairs and a window. I had a view of the town. I wondered who I displaced as I doubted such a fine office belonged to someone in an inferior position.

"Are you certain you don't have a smaller, plainer space for me?"

His shoulders dipped slightly, and his smile faded. "You don't like it?"

"I love it," I quickly reassured him.

As he explained my duties, I set my satchel on the floor near my chair. Then he led me over to the accounting depart-ment. He introduced me to a young man named Sidney Allen.

"Sidney is the contact for accounting. If you need information about invoices or need to make sure we apply the terms of a contract at time of payment, talk to him. I suspect that we have some room for improvement in communicating the terms of our contracts to the accounting depart-ment."

"Nice to meet you, Mr. Allen." I offered my hand to the short, thin man with kind brown eyes. He shook it.

"Please, call me Sid or Sidney. Mr. Colter and Mr. Murphy are the only men who are formal around here."

I stored away that piece of information.

James introduced me to the general counsel and then led me back to my office.

"I've asked Gerard to separate our new contracts from the older ones. Start with the new ones that arrive. As time permits, review the older contracts and work with Sidney to audit what the accounting department pays out."

I sat at my desk and reached for a new contract.

"It's good to have you here, Keri," James whispered.

"Good day, Mr. Colter," I said. If Sidney and others called him Mr. Colter, then I would too.

I caught his surprised look before he wiped it away. He turned and walked across the hall to his office.

After I picked the first contract from the stack, I took notes while I reviewed the contract. It was from a steel mill in the east. They shipped used rails to the SFP&P for the construction of the line between Ash Fork and Prescott.

I wondered if it was normal to send used rails or not. I made a note to discuss it with James later and to check with Sidney whether they billed us for new or used.

As the day wore on, my stomach growled. I looked at the clock. It was half past noon. I stood and stretched out the soreness from sitting too long. Then I left my office. Gerard wasn't at his desk, so I peered into James's office.

He looked up and smiled. "Can I help you?"

"Sorry, I didn't see Gerard and wondered if it's fine if I leave for lunch?"

He came around his desk. "Of course. I forgot to show you the cafeteria. The company provides lunch at no cost. Come."

He offered his arm, but I declined. We were not on a date. We were at work. Again, I saw his disappointment before he masked it.

"If you give me directions, I can find my way."

"Nonsense."

He took my hand and pulled me forward. After a few steps, he released my hand. I followed him down the grand staircase and into the cafeteria where workers sat at tables of four. Instead of menus and servers, we picked out what food items we wanted from a counter.

He placed his hand on the small of my back and guided me to the line. Clearly, I could not avoid a perception of special treatment when he was with me. The next day, I would sneak down for lunch without him.

I took a tray and requested a chicken salad sandwich, iced tea, and an apple. Without waiting for James, I found an open seat at a table. I introduced myself, but the men stood and moved to another table. I frowned.

James sat down on one of the newly vacated seats. "Have a seat."

I did begrudgingly as I worried about why the others left so quickly.

"How do you like it so far?"

I held back a sigh and answered his question before I asked, "Do we normally purchase used rails?"

"We've purchased both new and used rails. The steel mills inspect the used rails and if the integrity of the steel is good, they will send the used ones. Otherwise, they ship new ones. Why do you ask?"

"It looks like the steel mill back east sent used rails. Is that normal?"

"Do you think they billed us incorrectly?"

"I'm not sure. It's on my list of items to discuss with Sidney. When we receive the rails, can we tell if they are new or used?"

James thought for a moment. "Check with Daniel Parker, the superintendent of traffic. If he doesn't know, he can introduce you to the construction manager."

When I finished my sandwich and tea, I took my apple and stood.

"Please, don't rush off," James reached for my hand, but I dodged him.

"I'm sorry. There is much work to do. I'm sure you under-stand."

My heart pierced at the look of hurt on his face. I turned and hurried back to my office. I set the apple on my desk. Then I grabbed my notebook and headed over to talk to Sidney. He agreed to investigate the invoices. Then I found Daniel Parker's office.

He smiled warmly at me when I introduced myself.

"Yes, I remember seeing you on the excursion yesterday. Did you enjoy the picnic?"

My cheeks warmed. "Very much. The food was delicious. Where did it come from?"

"Our cafeteria cook prepared the baskets. Though, we may outsource that to a restaurant in town. How may I help you?"

I asked my questions about tracking used versus new rails. He walked me down the hall to the construction manager, who promised to examine it in the next few days. Before I returned to my office, I thanked both men for their help.

It was late in the day, so I gathered my things and headed home. As I stepped out onto the street, I heard James call my name from a window overhead.

"Keri, wait! I'll walk you home."

I nodded.

When he joined me, I walked next to him and did not accept his arm until we were out of sight of the office.

"You can't keep doing that," I said.

"Doing what?"

"Acting like I'm your sweetheart."

James turned his head toward me as we walked. "I thought we established that yesterday. You are."

I sighed. "I am. But not at work. Not if I hope to fit in. It's already difficult since I'm a woman attorney."

He wrapped his hand over mine as it rested in the crook of his arm. "I'm sorry I made it more difficult for you today. I love seeing and working with you every day."

My heart softened at his genuine enthusiasm. He really cared for me. I ought to be more understanding of his feelings.

"Would you like to join us for supper?" I asked as he escorted me to the door of my home. "I'm sure there will be plenty."

"Not tonight." He kissed my cheek. "My housekeeper will have something ready when I usually arrive home."

He faced me and ran a finger along my cheek. "I'll try to be less of a suitor at work."

I kissed his cheek. "Thank you. See you tomorrow."

CHAPTER 15

JAMES

By Wednesday, Keri and I fell into a routine. I tried to keep my relationship with her professional at work, which was difficult the more I learned about her. She was very talented and saved us thousands of dollars in the few short days she worked at the SFP&P. My admiration of her grew. My confidence that I would not have to pay her salary out of mine increased with each contract she reviewed.

Gerard knocked on my open door. "Sir, telegram that you need to see."

He handed it to me. As I read the words, my throat constricted.

"Has Frank seen this yet?"

"No sir."

I stood and hurried over to Frank's office. His door was closed, so I knocked.

"One minute!"

I cracked the door open. "You need to see this now."

Frank dismissed the Superintendent of Construction and motioned for me to enter. I handed him the telegram and paced the length of the room.

He launched to his feet. "Stock market crash?"

I nodded numbly. "It hit the railroad sector hard."

"We need more information. Wire Robinson to get details."

I left the room to give Gerard the message and asked him to wait for the response. Then I headed back to Frank's office.

"I should go," I said. "Meet with Robinson in Chicago."

"We should both go. But let's wait for his response."

"We should halt construction," I suggested.

"Let's wait until we talk with Robinson."

I sighed heavily. That was the worst news we could have received. Robinson's response wasn't better.

"Come at once," I read his response after Gerard left. "I don't understand why he didn't notify us the day it happened instead of three business days later."

Frank shook his head. "I don't know. It doesn't bode well."

I asked Gerard to secure accommodations for us in Chicago. Then I stopped by Keri's office.

"Do you have a minute?" I asked when she looked up. My heart warmed at her smile.

When she saw my concern, she frowned. "What's wrong?"

I closed the door behind me. Then I paced in front of her desk. "I have to go to Chicago. I'm afraid it is not good news. The stock market crashed. Railroad, lumber, and steel experienced significant losses. Frank and I must meet with the president of our line to discuss the impact and come up with a plan."

"Do you need me to come? Will there be changes to our contract with the A&P?"

"You can stay here. I'm not sure what changes we will

make."

"Are you sure you don't want me there? You know I will watch out for the SFP&P. If not me, consider taking Papa or the general counsel."

I ran a hand through my hair. Robinson would not approve it until we knew more.

"I appreciate it, Keri, but Frank and I need more information before we take any action."

When I moved around her desk to stand in front of her, I held out my hands, and she stood. Then I placed my hands on her waist. I let out a slow breath as I looked at the corner of the room, afraid my lifelong dream would crumble.

She placed a hand on my cheek. "Look at me."

I did.

"Everything will be fine. Trust your instincts. The SFP&P will weather this storm."

"I hope you're right."

Then I lowered my head and gave her a brief kiss before I released her. "I have to leave this afternoon. I'll see you next week or the week after."

"I'll pray for you, James," she said before I opened the door.

I gave her a curt nod. Then I hurried home to pack.

Frank and I caught the afternoon train. After arriving in Ash Fork, we continued on the A&P. We rode straight through the three-day journey with very little sleep. Even though we discussed options, none of our plans mattered until we spoke with Robinson.

By the time we arrived in Chicago, I was exhausted. We freshened up at the hotel before joining Robinson at his home for a private meal.

"Frank, James," he greeted us as we entered his mansion. It made my home in Prescott feel insignificant.

He led us to the dining room, where he waited until the servants left. Even his wife did not join us.

"It's not good," he said as he shook his head. "Banks are failing all over the country. The Philadelphia & Reading Railroad went into receivership earlier this year. The investors at the A&P are pulling back funds. We have to follow suit and halt all construction if we have any hope of weathering the storm."

Frank rubbed his chin. "Any other railroads in danger?"

"The Atchison, Topeka, & Santa Fe, for one. Northern Pacific is also on shaky ground."

My stomach clenched. Our railroad might die before it got off the ground. All my dreams teetered on a precipice.

"As soon as you get back, stop construction and lay off the construction workers," Robinson said. "We must reduce staff-ing across the board to essential workers only."

I took a sip of brandy to calm my lurching stomach. All those years of hard work, and it might be over soon because of forces outside of our control.

"European investors are fleeing the market," Robinson added. "Most railroads have benefited from European investors, so this loss will affect the entire sector."

"What about our obligations?" I asked. "And the A&Ps commitment to the town of Ash Fork?"

"They will finish the deliveries en route, then they will be done. They have no contractual obligation to the town," Robinson said.

My jaw twitched. I did not like breaking my word. Frank cautioned me not to say more, so I held my tongue.

We discussed more detailed plans throughout the evening and the next few days. By the weekend, we headed home.

Neither Frank nor I were ready to give up on the

SFP&P. We agreed to do the best we could to keep it from going under. In my mind, I resolved to forgo some or all my salary throughout the summer, if it would keep our railway alive.

We arrived in Prescott on the morning train on Monday. I dropped my things at my home, then I retrieved my horse from the livery before I headed straight for Iron Springs.

My brother, Boone, and his surveying team were there, along with hundreds of men on the construction crew. There were a dozen women cooks and laundresses as well.

I asked the construction site manager to gather everyone. Then I made the announcement.

"I am sorry to bring bad news," I said once the din of the construction equipment quieted.

"The stock market crashed on May third, and it hit the railroad sector very hard. The funds we were expecting from investors dried up, forcing us to halt all construction."

The construction manager's face turned ashen, and his mouth formed a thin line. Boone frowned at me. The other workers whispered.

"Please, quiet down. Let me finish!"

When they settled, I continued, "The SFP&P will pay the cost of your transportation to Phoenix, Wickenburg, or Prescott to find other employment. Though we hope things will improve, we can't take the risk of keeping you on. We will pay you wages through the end of business today. The construction manager will provide more details."

The men shouted angrily. I made my way to the manager's railcar to meet with him in private.

"Please continue to feed the men and women until the food supplies are gone. Use the funds I brought to coordinate the efforts to help them move. Then I expect you back in Prescott next Monday."

"Do I still have a job?" he asked.

I glanced at the corner of the room.

"That's what I thought. You go, Mr. Colter. Leave the hard part to me," he growled through gritted teeth.

As soon as I stepped out of the railcar, Boone pulled me aside.

"What's going on, James? I thought you contracted us for a few more weeks."

"It's like I said, the stock market crashed. Our investors pulled their funding. If we hope to stay in business, major cuts are required."

He crossed his arms over his broad chest and looked down at me. "I trusted your word. I have a wife and child to provide for."

"Believe me, this is the last thing I wanted to do. This railroad is my dream. I'm just doing what is necessary to keep it alive."

Boone stalked off as my stomach turned.

The severity of layoffs was obvious to me. I was destroying the livelihood of hundreds of families, just like Boone's.

I mounted my horse, Brass, and headed down the mountain to Wickenburg. The conversation was as difficult the second time. By the time we were done, we displaced over one thousand men and women. I knew many would not find new jobs. It would force them to move beyond the few towns where we could send them.

Lord, please help these people.

I spent the night in Wickenburg before returning to Prescott the next morning.

When I arrived in the office around lunchtime, my duties required more cuts. I asked our human resources manager, Fred, to gather a list of employees. Then Frank, Fred, and I discussed which positions were essential to keep the line running between Prescott and Ash Fork.

"Your sweetheart needs to go, James," Frank said.

I frowned. "She has already saved us thousands of dollars. If we keep her on, there's a strong likelihood she will save us more."

Frank narrowed his eyes. "James—"

"I'm serious. If she can save us thousands more, paying her a meager salary will be worth every penny."

"I'll give you until the end of the week then she must go."

My jaw tightened. I wanted to fight for her. "Frank—"

"Enough. It's not negotiable. Essential workers only. That means one person in accounting. One secretary, that would be Gerard. The Superintendent of Transportation. The bulk of the transportation department all need to stay. We have to get the budget down to five hundred dollars a month."

My throat constricted. That was a minuscule fraction of our labor cost.

"You and I are not drawing a salary until this is over."

I nodded numbly. I agreed to his stipulation on the way back from Chicago, but only out of desperation to save my dream.

"Do I have your word that Keri will be gone on Friday?"

"Yes," I replied through clenched teeth. I hoped she would forgive me.

CHAPTER 16

KERI

James made himself scarce the week he returned from Chicago after laying off the entire construction crew. Finally on Friday, he came into my office.

"Hi," he mumbled as he dropped onto a chair across from my desk. No smile. He rubbed the back of his neck and his gaze darted to the window.

"James," I said warmly and smiled. "I've missed you."

His gaze jumped back to mine briefly, then he frowned and let out a long sigh. "I can't tell you how wonderful it's been to have you here. I love seeing you at work."

"I enjoy seeing you too," I said I as fidgeted with a paper on my desk.

"What you've done for us has exceeded my expectations. You've saved us so much money." His eyes looked anywhere but at me.

"But?" I shuffled the papers on my desk. Then I sat up straighter.

Finally, he looked me in the eye. "I have to let you go, but I don't want to. Frank gave me no choice."

I shook my head. "You just hired me."

He leaned forward and reached for my hand. I swiped it away and frowned.

"James." I blinked.

"I'm so sorry. I wish I could keep you. You could save us more."

"I can."

Slowly, I stood and grabbed my satchel, ready to storm out of the office, but he stood and blocked my exit.

"Keri." His voice was soft. He placed his hands on my arms and stooped to look at me. "This doesn't change how I feel about you. I love you and want to keep seeing you. I know this hurts."

I twisted away from his hold as my indignation rose. "Hurt? Of course, it hurts. I barely had enough time to prove that I'm a good contract attorney. You, James, asked me to work here."

He ran a hand through his hair. "If it makes you feel any better, I am working for no pay."

My eyes widened. "You are not drawing a salary?"

He shook his head. "It's not fair to displace so many people and still accept a wage. If I want this railroad to survive, then I need to do this."

"This, as in not getting paid? Or not keeping me?"

"Both."

I put my hand on his chest and pushed him out of my way. As I stepped forward, he grasped my arm.

"Please don't leave angry. Let me take you to dinner. Talk to me."

My eyes burned as the emotion pushed to the surface. James, my beau, ripped away the job that would prove I was as capable as any man.

I froze but kept my face forward.

"Keri, please."

"I need." My voice cracked. I shook off his hold. "To be alone."

Then I hurried down the grand staircase and out the front door. Tears trickled down my cheeks as I wandered.

Three weeks. That must be the shortest job in the history of my family. How embarrassing. I couldn't go home. I couldn't face Papa. He would be so disappointed.

In the town square, I sat down on a bench as I watched people walk home. James's brother Boone closed his office across the street for the evening. His shoulders slumped. I wondered if James fired him, too.

After fetching my handkerchief, I dabbed my eyes. Hundreds of employees lost their jobs, not just me. At least I had a family that could provide for me. I ought to be thankful.

"May I sit?"

I closed my eyes and nodded. Then James sat next to me. He placed his arm around my shoulders as his lips pressed against the top of my head.

The tears came again. I loved that job and excelled at it. I made a difference. The pain of losing it would linger for some time.

As we sat on the bench, I said nothing. Neither did James. He held me and let me cry for several minutes.

"Would you care for some supper?" he asked.

As I dabbed at my eyes, I nodded.

He stood and held out his hand. He carried my satchel over his shoulder. Then he clasped my hand in his and escorted me to a nearby restaurant where he requested a table near the back.

Once we ordered, he started the conversation.

"I know this hurts, Keri. My heart is breaking. Nearly one thousand employees lost their jobs this week alone.

Frank and I are foregoing our salaries. We hope these steep cuts will keep the SFP&P solvent."

I felt terrible. I never considered how much greater his hurt was. He delivered the bad news to so many people. His dream was in danger of dissolving. I reached across the table and squeezed his hand.

He looked at me. "I'm hopeful we won't have to take more extreme measures in the coming weeks and months. A lot of it depends on how the stock market recovers and if we can convince investors that our line is worth the investment."

"It must be hard to see your dream in dire straits," I whispered.

He took a sip of his iced tea. "More than I can say. I've worked towards this goal for ten years. I've sacrificed other dreams to achieve this one."

"Other dreams?"

He cleared his throat. "A wife. A family of my own."

He waited for the server to deliver our food before he continued. "I once believed I didn't dream of those things. Since meeting you, I've realized how incredibly lonely I am. I couldn't bear if you hated me or rebuffed me because of this."

"I'm here, aren't I?"

"Thank you."

As I wasn't sure what else to say, I bit into my food. I was still disappointed about losing my job and I felt for him and all he lost. Still, I loved him. Or at least I thought it could be love. I wasn't sure. All I knew was that I didn't want to lose him, either.

When we finished, he walked me home. At the bottom of the porch, he turned me to him.

"Thank you for staying with me." He placed his hands

on my waist and pulled me close. His voice was husky when he spoke. "I don't want to lose you."

Then he lifted a hand and caressed my neck before he lowered his lips to mine. He searched almost desperately. As I looped my arms around his neck, he pressed me even closer and deepened the kiss. His hands roamed over my back, which ignited a craving in my soul.

"Ahem."

My papa's voice broke through to my brain and I abruptly jumped back from James as if his clothing suddenly burst into flames. I rubbed the back of my hand across my lips.

James winked at me. Then he handed me my satchel.

"Good night, Keri. Alex."

"James." Papa's greeting held a warning.

"I'll see you at church on Sunday."

"Good night, James."

He walked backwards for a few steps with a smile just for me before he turned and headed home.

"Inside young lady."

As I entered the parlor, I set my satchel on a chair. I glanced at Mama, who frowned.

"To the den."

I bit the inside of my cheek as I followed Papa to his den. Once we were inside, he closed the door behind him.

"I'm guessing you had supper?"

"Yes. James took me out after he fired me."

Papa's frown softened. "You lost your job?"

I nodded. "So did hundreds of other employees."

"So, it's true." He leaned on his elbows and tented his hands together. "I heard rumors it might happen."

I shrugged. "Well, I was one of the many."

Papa sighed. "I'm sorry. I know how much you liked

that job."

"If you want me back at the law office, I'm available."

"There's plenty of work."

He cleared his throat. "About James. If you will not be at supper, you need to send word. Or come home to let us know. Your mother was frantic."

"Understood."

"And the—um—embrace I witnessed." He cleared his throat again. "Be careful. That looked pretty serious from where I stood."

I glanced at the painting on his wall. It was one of Grandpa's ranch in the spring. Papa painted it years ago. The scene calmed me and was my favorite of all his paintings.

"We love each other," I said.

Papa sighed. "I thought that might happen. Just be careful. Don't go to his house unchaperoned. Keep your wits about you on our front porch or on the street or wherever else the two of you steal kisses."

I looked at Papa. "So, you're not mad?"

"My feelings won't change how you feel about him. I have a strong suspicion if I forbade you to kiss him or whatever, it would just drive you to do it more. So, I'm asking you to be wise."

"Yes, Papa."

I stood and walked to the door.

"You're lucky I caught you, you know. If your mother saw that, I think she may have shipped you off to a convent."

He winked at me.

As I closed the door behind me, I smiled. I carefully wiped it away when I joined Mama in the parlor to give her the short version of my day before I took my satchel up to my room.

Then I fell backwards onto my bed. I loved James. He loved me. At least the day ended on a rosy note.

CHAPTER 17

JAMES

A month passed while I worked for no salary at the SFP&P. Our income from new freight contracts increased. Passenger service was sluggish, but our picnic excursion was a tremendous success. Somehow, we made it through still solvent with no additional layoffs. By the third week of June, I was relieved that we survived the financial panic to that point.

I studied the paperwork in front of me but failed to concentrate. My family wanted to celebrate my birthday on Sunday. I sighed. I wanted to bring Keri, except I worried that my family might make it into more than it was. We were courting, not engaged.

"James? I hoped I might find you here."

I looked up and Mama greeted me with a warm smile.

"Good morning, Mama." I smiled as I stood to hug her. "What brings you by?"

"You missed Sam's birthday," she said as she took a seat across from my desk. I sat in the chair next to her and angled it so I could see her clearly.

"I assumed I would not be welcome."

Mama sighed heavily. "I wish the two of you would put this nonsense behind you. What is done is done. There's a railroad through a tiny corner of our land."

"Mama, I'm not the one who is holding a grudge."

She took my hand in hers and patted it before releasing it. "I know. If you had come for his birthday, it would have made it harder for him to stay angry with you."

"I suppose. Unfortunately, I traveled that weekend."

Mama held my gaze for a few seconds. Her shoulders slumped for a moment before she straightened her back.

"Come out this Sunday after church, so we can celebrate your birthday."

I shifted my eyes to the window. "Will it be at the ranch house?" Sam and his wife and children took over the main ranch house earlier in the year as Preston hadn't lived there for over a year. Deacon and Grady took over the Cahill home when Warren left the ranch to start his own near Congress. Only Vi lived at home with Mama and Papa, so they moved into the smaller original cabin ranch house.

"Of course. Ellie Mae is happy to host. It's still the family home and the only place large enough to accommodate us all."

"Is Sam happy to host?"

Mama sighed. "Your father did not give him a choice."

As I thought. It would be awkward and tense.

"Please, James. It will be the beginning of healing the rift between you. Besides, I miss you terribly. You hardly ever come out anymore. And you haven't brought Keri out yet."

There it was. She knew I was courting Keri. The entire town knew it because I sat with her in church every week. Certainly, all the hopeful young women mourned that the most eligible bachelor in town, me, chose Keri.

"Should I bring her with me if I come? I would hate for

her to be snubbed because Sam won't bury the hatchet."

Mama frowned. "Regardless of Sam's feelings toward you, he won't treat her poorly. He's not that way. And Ellie Mae has been dying to meet her. Vi is so excited to see her friend again."

I forgot Vi was close friends with Keri and her sister Sadie.

"We'll come."

"Excellent. I'll see if George and Maggie want to join us. I'm sure they would like the opportunity to catch up with their granddaughter."

I nodded. "I'll see you after church on Sunday."

Mama stood and hugged me before she left.

My stomach knotted. Knowing George Larson's penchant for romanticism, the Larsons were going to see me bringing Keri as a very serious thing. It wasn't.

I swiveled my chair to face the window.

Maybe it was more serious than I wanted to admit. Over the past few weeks, I took Keri on several dates. Sometimes we walked around the town square in the evening or in her neighborhood. Other times I took her to supper or lunch. I rarely traveled since I returned from Chicago in mid-May. So, I spent time with her most days.

Yet, she and her parents offered no invitations to supper. I wondered if that was her mother's doing. My attempts to win her over were unsuccessful. I was confident Mel would not appreciate her parents being invited to my birthday with Keri on my arm.

I left work early that afternoon and headed over to their law office. Alex's secretary greeted me when I entered.

"Mr. Colter, I don't have you on the schedule for today."

"I'm here to see Keri. Is she available?"

"One moment."

He motioned me to the waiting area. Within a few minutes, Keri entered.

"James, this is a surprise." The excitement in her eyes made me feel like I was the most important man in the world.

I kissed her on the cheek. "Would you care to go out for supper tonight?"

"I'm sorry, I can't. Would you like to join us instead?"

My throat constricted. "Is your mother agreeable to it?"

"Of course." Her high-pitched tone betrayed her lack of confidence.

"Perhaps some other time."

I reached for her hand. "Can you spare a few minutes for a walk?"

She smiled and took my hand. I ushered her outside and across the street to the town square where we sat on a bench facing the courthouse.

"My birthday is Monday. Mama stopped by to see if we will join them for supper after church on Sunday to celebrate."

Keri pouted. "You didn't tell me it was your birthday."

I held back a sigh. "I'm sorry. My birthday is not something I like to celebrate."

"Oh." She angled to face me. "Why not?"

"Honestly? I am reminded of the one area of life where I have been the most unsuccessful." I immediately regretted the words.

"And that would be?"

"It's hard to watch my younger brothers fall in love and marry. Some days I wonder if I will be the last to wed."

She reached for my hand. "You don't see marriage as a possibility for us?"

Her blue eyes searched mine. She bit her lower lip and

held her breath.

I reached up and let my fingers caress the length of her neck. Then I pulled her face close to mine. My lips lightly brushed hers before I rested my forehead against hers. "What do you think?"

Her breath warmed my lips as she spoke. "I... um..."

I turned up one side of my mouth in a smile. "Speechless?"

The air between us ignited the longer I lingered there. The truth I avoided saying out loud was that I could see marriage with her. At the right time, I would say so. Just not then.

She angled her head and closed the distance that separated our lips. Her movements were tentative at first, but as I wrapped my arms around her, she became bolder, which triggered a longing and desire in me. I hoped those kisses were enough to answer her question.

When she released her hold and sat up straighter. She cleared her throat. "What were we talking about?"

I smiled. "How we're going to the ranch on Sunday after church for supper? Your grandparents will be there as well."

"Hmm, yes. That was it."

I grinned before I stood and escorted her back to the law office.

As I walked home, I made a mental note to keep my thoughts about marriage to myself until I was ready for something more.

———

After church on Sunday, I rented a carriage for the drive to the ranch. She carried a small package with her. I figured it was a gift for my birthday. It seemed awkward to receive a gift from her when I gave her nothing. I would remedy that next week.

As we crested the last hill overlooking the ranch, she sighed. "This is my favorite part of the ride. Seeing the entire place in one sweeping view. I have such fond memories here."

I hoped that day would be another fond memory, though I doubted it, given the animosity with Sam.

I pulled the carriage around to the front of the ranch house. Ellie Mae smiled as she opened the door.

"Welcome! Keri, we are so glad you could join us."

I helped Keri down. Then walked her to the front door. Ellie Mae pulled her into a hug before giving me a quick hug.

"James. So glad to have you here. Happy Birthday."

"James." The flatness in Sam's tone did not bode well for a family meal. He offered his hand for a shake. I shook his hand and pulled him closer for a pat on the back, as I hoped it satisfied Mama that I did my best to mend fences. Sam patted my back, then quickly released his hold.

Deacon and Grady rounded the side of the house. They both greeted me and Keri. Then Grady offered to take care of the horse and carriage. I was relieved, as I did not like the idea of leaving Keri alone with Sam and his lackluster welcome.

When we entered the house, the rest of my family greeted me. A second table stood in the parlor for Sam's two boys, daughter, and Boone's son. I wondered how that would pan out, given Boone's son and Sam's daughter were a little over one year old. Then I noticed Vi and Jaclyn took seats with the children.

Keri hugged George and Maggie Larson. Then I greeted them before I held a chair for Keri to sit across from

Maggie. I sat across from George.

After Papa blessed the meal, Ellie Mae said, "On a happy note, we are expecting another child."

Jaclyn turned to face her. "When?"

"Thanksgiving time frame. Maybe early December, I think."

"Congratulations," Jaclyn said as she bounced Jaxson on her knee.

Ellie Mae's cheeks turned pink. Keri offered her congratulations as well.

"So," Ellie Mae continued, "Tell us the story of how you two met."

Keri laughed. "That's boring. We met on this very ranch as children."

Ellie Mae laughed.

George jumped in. "You know what your grandpa wants to hear. How did you fall in love?"

"And when?" Maggie asked.

I shifted in my chair before I glanced at Keri.

"It's hard to know where to start," Keri said. "Over the years, we've met on several occasions. I suppose the most recent one, which led to us courting, was when James invited me on the inaugural trip for the SFP&P."

"The first encounter," I added, "was at a dance two years ago." I remembered the night well. The way she looked in that dress, and how she flirted with me. How wonderful she felt in my arms as we danced.

She smiled at me. "Yes, I suppose you could count that as when we first met."

CHAPTER 18

KERI

I loved recounting our story to James's family and my grandparents. Grandpa plied me with several questions throughout the meal.

After the meal, as the family retired to the parlor, Grandpa asked me how long I loved James.

"It's hard to pinpoint it. The dance," I kept my voice low so only he and Grandma could hear, "was magical. Yet, I was only sixteen, so it may not have been love."

Grandma smiled. "Aye. It might have been the beginning of it."

"I think by the end of the initial train ride, I knew. The fire at Ash Fork brought us close."

Grandma patted my hand. "We think it is wonderful."

I frowned. "I wish Mama did."

Grandpa quirked an eyebrow. "What issue could Melissa possibly have? Our families have been friends for generations. James is an honest, hardworking man."

I smoothed out my skirt, then fidgeted with it. "She thinks he's too old."

Grandma laughed. "If that isn't the pot calling the kettle."

Grandpa smiled. "Give her time. You're the oldest."

I rolled my eyes. "I know. I get to pave the way for my siblings."

Just then, Hannah got everyone's attention and suggested we give James our gifts. Boone and his wife went first. Ellie Mae was second, while Sam frowned the entire time. Deacon and Grady were up next. Then Will and Hannah.

Finally, my gift was the only one left. I stood and walked across the room. I handed him the small package.

"I know you have everything you could need or want. But when I saw these, they reminded me of you."

He smiled as he took the package. He quirked an eyebrow as he pulled on the string. Then he opened the small box to reveal the eagle's head cuff links. It was an expensive gift. Judging by the awe on his face, he recognized that.

James stood and kissed me on the cheek. "Thank you."

"You handle a crisis with confidence, and you project assurance and tenacity. The eagle seemed to fit."

"I love them." His broad smile warmed my heart.

A loud noise came from behind me.

"George!" Grandma shouted. "George!"

When I turned around, I saw grandpa on the floor. Hannah leaped to her feet to help him. She loosened his collar. Deacon thrust a black bag toward her.

"Ride out for the doctor," she told him. Deacon sprinted out of the house.

"What's going on?" My voice sounded distant as my legs felt weak.

James placed an arm around my waist and led me to a chair. I couldn't see Grandpa's face. His body went limp. Grandma cried over him.

"Help me get him on the couch," Hannah said.

Boone and Grady lifted him onto the furniture. His face looked ashen. The side of his mouth drooped.

"James, what is happening?"

"I don't know. Mama will help," he whispered in my ear.

My eyes burned as my throat constricted. I worried he might die right there. I turned my face away and buried it against James's chest.

"Let's get some air," he suggested.

I nodded and followed him to the porch. He motioned for me to sit in a rocking chair. Then he sat beside me and took my hand in his. He closed his eyes and his lips moved silently. Prayer. Yes, I ought to pray.

Only words would not form in my mind or heart. Some-thing was terribly wrong, and I felt helpless. I sat there and stared at the lake.

Will rushed past us. A few minutes later, he came back with Uncle Adam and Aunt Julia.

After some length of time, Hannah stepped onto the porch.

"He's sleeping," she said. "The doctor will tell us more."

It was another hour before Deacon returned with the doctor. James moved us back into the house to the dining room table. Boone and Jaclyn headed home with their son. Ellie Mae took her children upstairs when it happened. Grady returned to his home on the property. Vi came over and sat beside me. She said nothing and just held my hand.

When the doctor finished examining Grandpa, he explained what he thought had happened.

"I believe he had a stroke. He needs to stay in town for a while."

Grandma nodded. "I want to come too."

"Grandma, you can stay with us," I said. "You can have

my room."

She turned to me and patted my cheek. "Thank you. That would be nice."

"Let's pack some things for you and Grandpa," I said as I stood.

"We'll drive him into town in the wagon," Uncle Adam said.

Then he left and followed James to the barn as I led Grandma to her home on the property.

"Let's bring a few changes of clothes and some night-clothes," I suggested.

Grandma led me to their bedroom. Then she laid out another outfit for each of them. I found a valise and careful-ly placed the items in it. Then I gathered Grandpa's groom-ing supplies and added them to the bag.

When I felt like we had what they needed for the short term, I carried the valise and helped Grandma to the Colter's home.

Adam volunteered to drive the wagon so he could bring it back home after they got Grandpa to the doctor's office. Grandma insisted on riding in the back of the wagon with him. I set their valise in the carriage and rode with James back to town.

"We should stop by your home," he suggested. "Your mother will want to know right away."

"So will Papa. And my brothers and sisters."

James pulled the carriage to a stop in front of my house. He carried the valise in and set it down as I explained to my family what happened.

"Grandpa had a stroke." My voice cracked as Mama gasped and tears instantly pooled in the corner of her eyes. "Adam is taking him to the doctor's office now. Grandma is with him. I brought a few things for them. She can have my room, and I'll share with Sadie and Amelia."

My sisters nodded their agreement despite their tears.

Papa's face looked pale. "Will you stay with your brothers and sisters?"

I nodded.

"Take the carriage," James offered. "I can return it to Anderson's Livery in the morning."

"Thank you," Mama said as she squeezed James's hand and then hugged me.

Papa hurried her out the door.

I sank into the closest chair and let out a long breath. James hovered nearby.

"Will Grandpa be alright?" Amelia asked.

I opened my arms to offer a hug. She climbed onto my lap. I held her close and stroked her hair. "We will pray so."

James leaned down and kissed the top of my head. "I'll be back soon. Your aunts need notified. I'll wire Georgie and Helen too."

"You don't have to do that."

"I want to." He nodded and left.

Amelia fell asleep on my lap, so I carried her upstairs to her room. Then I returned to the parlor.

"Is anyone hungry?"

The boys nodded. Sadie declined.

I asked the cook to bring out a tray. She fixed sandwiches for the boys and other family, in case any showed up. Then I returned to the parlor.

My brothers were unusually quiet as we waited for news. When the cook brought sandwiches, they each ate one. I nibbled on a sandwich. Sadie stared out the window.

"James is back." She stood and opened the door.

He entered and sat next to me on the couch. "Caroline went to the doctor's office to stay with your grandma.

Bethie couldn't leave the children, as Hawk is out of town. She said she sends her love and is praying."

I nodded numbly.

"I wired Georgie and Helen to let them both know we'll send word as soon as we know more."

"Thank you."

He placed his arm around my shoulders. I leaned against him for strength, and I eventually fell asleep.

When I woke after midnight, James sat in a chair nearby. My siblings had already retired to their rooms.

"James," I said as I yawned. "You don't have to stay."

He smiled softly. "I'll wait with you."

"Alright." I glanced at the clock. "Happy birthday. Sorry, it didn't turn out like you might have hoped."

Before he could respond, the door opened. Papa, Mama, and Grandma entered the house. They looked drained. I stood and hugged Grandma and Mama.

James stood and told Papa that he notified everyone.

"Thank you for doing that," Papa said.

"How is he?" I asked.

"Resting," Papa said. "The doctor wants to keep him there for a few days."

Then I showed James to the door. He gave me a light kiss on the lips before he left. Then I showed Grandma to my room. I grabbed a few things and went into my sister's room. Sweet Sadie shared a bed with Amelia and left me her bed. I changed and fell into the bed as weariness washed over me.

CHAPTER 19

JAMES

Monday morning, my actual birthday, felt like it started earlier than normal. Perhaps it was the late night and stress as I worried about Keri and her family, especially George.

One minute, he laughed and teased his granddaughter. The next, he collapsed onto the floor in a heap. It sobered me. Life could end in an instant. I vowed to make the most of the time God granted me. My priorities changed.

I walked to the office mid-morning. When I entered my office, Frank cornered me.

"Did you see what Bullock did?"

I shook my head.

"He sliced his rates so low that our customers are crawling back to him, even though they despise him."

"How low are we talking?" I asked as I frowned.

"Eight percent below ours."

I coughed and pounded my chest with a fist as I plopped onto my chair. "We can't counter that."

"I know, but we must. Otherwise, the railway may fold in a month."

"What does Robinson say?"

Frank frowned and shook his head. "Can't reach him. So, this is my decision."

I frowned and leaned forward on my desk. As I let out a long breath, I rubbed my temples with my fingers.

"It's not surprising," Frank said. "He's practically the Pres-ident in name only."

"What are you going to do?"

"We're going to drop prices by eight and a half percent, then see what happens."

"Alright. I'll get Mr. Parker on it right away."

Frank stood and returned to his office.

I headed over to Daniel Parker's office.

"Mr. Colter, an eight and a half percent cut is too much. There are contracts where we will lose money on each shipment at that rate."

My gut tightened. "Make a list of those customers. Then I'll review it with Frank."

Within an hour, Daniel provided the list. Frank wanted to proceed, so I approved the new pricing. I hoped Frank knew what he was doing. I thought it was an insane strate-gy. If we kept pace with Bullock's reductions, both lines might go out of business.

Late in the afternoon, I finally escaped and headed over to see Keri.

When I knocked on the door, no one answered. I knocked again, and the housekeeper answered the door. A loud racket came from down the hall towards Alex's den. Despite the housekeeper's instruction to stay in the parlor, I walked down the hall.

"Stand it on its end," Alex said.

"Hello!" I announced my presence. "Need some help?"

Alex looked up. "James. Yes. The boys are trying to help, but we would appreciate another set of hands."

I removed my jacket and laid it over a chair in the dining room. Then I rolled up my sleeves.

"We need to tilt the desk up on its end," Alex said. "George and Maggie are staying with us, so I'm moving my office to the parlor."

Alex and I hefted it up on one side. Then we shimmied it through the doorway.

Perspiration dotted my forehead. "Can we set it down?" I asked halfway down the hall.

We did, and Alex exhaled loudly. "This beast is heavier than I thought."

"Where are we going with this?"

"The area of the parlor past the staircase."

I held back a sigh. It was the furthest corner of the parlor. "Ready?"

Alex grunted as he lifted his side. I did the same. We took another break by the staircase before we finally set it in place and tilted it back to its normal position.

I dabbed the sweat off my forehead with my handkerchief.

"Glad you came by when you did." Alex shook my hand. "I think the boys and I can manage the rest of it."

"I'm here and already a little mussed, so might as well put me to work."

He slapped me on the shoulder, and we went back to the den again. Over the next hour, Alex, me, Clinton, and Archie moved the office furniture into the parlor. Alex assured me they would move all the books from the floor of his den after supper.

"Keri and Mel should be home soon. Will you join us for supper?" he asked. "It's the least I can do to repay you."

I smiled. "If I might trouble you for a chance to freshen up first."

He showed me to the washroom upstairs. I splashed some water on my face. Then I carefully removed my shirt ran a damp cloth over my arms and chest. Then I dressed again. I twitched at the sight of wrinkles in my sleeves as I unrolled them. It was for a good cause.

When I descended the stairs, Keri entered the house. She smiled and hurried to greet me.

"James!" She hugged me tight for a few seconds before she released me. I kissed her on the cheek.

"How is George?"

Her smile faded. "Not good."

I motioned for her to sit, and then I took a chair near her.

"He can't speak. His entire right side is immobile. The doctor thinks he might regain some functions, but not all. He will need…" She sniffed. "Full time care."

"I'm sorry."

"They are moving into Papa's den."

"I figured when I arrived, and your father was trying to move it himself. Well, with the help of your brothers."

"Mama told him to hire someone to help. The boys are too small for that."

I winked at her. "How much should I charge him?"

"You helped?"

"I left early, hoping to spend some time with you."

Her cheeks turned pink. "Mama and I went out to the ranch. We packed for Grandma and Grandpa."

"Do you have things to unpack?"

"No. Adam is going to bring some of your brothers and cowboys tomorrow to move furniture."

She let out a long breath and stared out the nearest window. Then she snapped her fingers. "In an instant, our lives turned upside down. Especially Grandma and Grandpa's."

"How is Maggie?"

Her eyes reddened with unshed tears. "Heartbroken. She's trying to put on a brave face for him."

I reached over and squeezed her hand.

"Supper is ready," Alex said, as he poked his head into the parlor.

Keri's siblings bustled into the dining room along with her mother. When she stood, I pulled her close for a brief kiss. I could only imagine what she and her family were going through.

Then I escorted her back to the dining room. Alex sat at the head of the table. He offered me the seat to his right across from Mel. Judging by her frown, she still hadn't warmed up to me.

After Alex said the blessing, the conversation buzzed.

"I see you and the boys moved everything," Mel said.

"James did the hardest work," Clinton said. "And Papa, of course."

Mel's expression remained stoic, but one eyebrow raised.

"Couldn't have done it without him," Alex affirmed.

Mel's lips twitched. I decided she wanted to smile but wouldn't.

"How is the railroad business?" Alex asked as Keri's siblings spoke at the other end of the table.

I swallowed a long swig of overly sweet tea. "We're locked in a rate war with Bullock now. That, the tightening of investors, and the massive layoffs... I'm concerned."

Alex frowned.

"James isn't drawing a salary either," Keri said.

I held back a cringe.

"Keri, that is none of our business," Mel said sharply, though her facial features softened some.

"I'm sorry," Keri said. "I thought you should know he's a

man of character."

I squeezed her hand for a few seconds before I sliced off another piece of roast.

"I already knew that," Alex said. "From our years of working together. Your mama knows that too." He winked at his wife.

Mel let out a sigh. "I do."

Happily, I accepted her acknowledgment. I could work with that.

"Have you kept up to date with the news about the World's Fair?" Keri asked.

As a distant memory came to mind, I swallowed a bite of food. I promised to take her. Thankfully, Alex picked up the conversation.

"I heard it opened in May and that the papers are calling it the Columbian Exposition. I wonder how the stock market crash has affected it."

"From what I've read, it continues as planned." I snorted. "Parts of it are still under construction."

"It must be amazing," Keri said. "Remember when we saw the site?"

I nodded.

"Mama, the area was immense. I read it's lit with electricity at night. How spectacular!"

"I wish we could go," I said before I thought better of it. "Unfortunately, now is terrible timing at the railroad."

Keri's eyes glittered with hope.

Mel's eyes shot daggers. "Keri, you aren't going. The sooner you accept it, the better."

Keri winked at me. I shifted in my chair, uncertain what she was thinking.

"October is several months away, so I'm not giving up hope yet. It's a once-in-a-lifetime opportunity."

I considered her words. October was a long time away. Perhaps, if things settled down with the railroad in another month, I could fulfill my promise.

Alex changed the subject. "Are you going to the Independence Day Ball on the fourth?"

As I finished the last bite of my meal, I set down my silverware. Like other prominent men in town, I received an invitation, but during the events of the last few days, I forgot about it.

I turned toward Keri. "What do you say? Shall we go?"

A smile stretched across her lips. "I would like that."

"Then we will go."

Mel's frown returned, and I held back a sigh.

Alex smiled. "Excellent. We are going as well. I do hope you will permit me at least one dance with my daughter."

"Of course."

Following supper, I joined the family in the parlor. I sat near Keri, and we spoke in hushed tones to keep our conversation as private as possible.

"Keri," I started. "Please don't share with others that I'm not drawing a salary. If word got out, it could damage public opinion of the railway. We could lose investors."

She bit her lip. "I'm sorry. You're right. I should not have mentioned it. I'm just at a loss how to change my mother's opinion."

I let out a long sigh. "Perhaps on the fourth, while your father claims his dance with you, I should speak with her."

Keri glanced at her mother. "That is a good idea. With Grandma moving in, I may enlist her help as well."

"About the World's Fair," I started. Her eyes sparkled with hope. "Would your parents even permit you to go with me?"

"They shouldn't be surprised we want to go together.

We are courting."

I ran a finger along the neck of my shirt. "That's true. However, I am sure they would insist on a chaperone."

"Leave that to me." She schooled her features. "If you want to take me—"

"I do. The earliest we can leave is September or October."

A soft smile stretched across her beautiful pink lips. "I will make sure they are comfortable with it."

Even though she was good at arguing her cause, I doubted Mel would ever agree to us traveling without a chaperone. I also questioned if Alex or Mel would make the trip, especially with Mel's parents moving into their home and George's poor health.

Keri reached over and patted my hand. Then I stood, and she walked me to the door.

"Good night, my love," I said as I placed a chaste kiss on her lips.

"Good night." She closed the door behind me.

My mind whirled as I walked home. I vowed to make the trip to the World's Fair happen, no matter what. If I had to pay someone to travel with us, I would. It was important to Keri, so it was important to me.

A vacation might do me good. I couldn't recall a single time where I traveled purely for my enjoyment. I only traveled for railroad business or to visit my family.

My spirits lifted, and hope ignited in my heart. No matter what the coming months threw at me and the railroad, I could handle it, since I looked forward to the trip with the woman I loved.

CHAPTER 20

KERI

The week after Grandpa's stroke, neither Mama nor I worked at the office. We coordinated the effort to move them into Papa's den. We tried to make it feel like their home and their space.

On Thursday, Uncle Adam brought Deacon Colter, Grady Thatcher, and a few cowboys from the ranch with a wagon load full of furniture and belongings.

"How is he?" Uncle Adam asked Mama when he arrived.

"About the same. He's more alert but struggles to communicate. He can't move most of his right side. We've purchased a wheeled chair for him so Mama or one of us can move him around easily."

Mama's words hit my heart. Grandpa was no longer independent. I couldn't picture it in my mind. Grandpa was always full of energy and life.

Deacon and Grady carried my grandparents' bed back to the den. Mama issued orders about the placement. The cowboys positioned the nightstands on each side of the bed. A dresser went along the wall under the large window. I stood on a chair and hung Grandma's curtains on the window. It was so large that I had to use two sets of matching curtains to cover its length.

The men stacked crates full of their belongings and trunks of their clothing. Mama purchased a wardrobe for Grandma's dresses, so when the men finished unloading the wagon, Adam picked it up from the store and brought it into the room.

The rest of the afternoon, Mama and I unpacked their things. It seemed strange to hang Grandma's dresses in a wardrobe in Papa's den.

I sighed heavily.

"What's wrong?" Mama asked.

"I'm glad that we can help Grandma and Grandpa, but it breaks my heart that he is so unwell."

Mama sniffed. "Mine too."

She stopped folding clothes and sat on the edge of the bed.

"I'm not ready to think about my papa... Passing."

"Oh, Mama!" I sat next to her and hugged her.

For the first time in days, my strong, unshakable mama finally cried. I rocked her back and forth as my own tears moistened my cheeks.

"It's made life seem so fragile. At night, I wonder how long Alex and I will have together. Will I one day be moving into your house or Sadie's, and you will care for me?"

My breath caught. "Mama don't think like that. We don't know how long we have. We don't know what will happen. Worrying about it will steal your joy from today."

Mama patted her cheeks dry with her handkerchief. "When did my daughter become so wise?"

She turned and gave me a half smile.

"For years now. I have two excellent role models."

I squeezed her shoulders and stood to finish unpacking

their things.

By four o'clock, Mama and I created a homey and wel-
coming room for them. When Papa brought them home
from the doctor's office, Grandpa was in the wheeled chair.
Papa huffed as he struggled to get the chair up the porch
stairs.

"Perhaps we should have someone build a ramp," Mama
suggested.

Papa grunted as he pulled the wheeled chair onto the
porch. "Good idea."

He wheeled Grandpa back to his new room. Grandma
followed behind.

"Oh, it's lovely!" Grandma exclaimed. "Melissa, Keri,
thank you so much. It feels like home."

The left side of Grandpa's lips twitched.

"I think Grandpa is smiling," I said.

He blinked twice in response.

"George," Papa said, "do you want to sit up for a while
or rest in bed?"

"Alex, only one question at a time," Grandma suggested.

"Right. Sorry. Bed?"

Grandpa made no movement.

"Sit up?"

Grandpa blinked twice.

"Alright."

Papa wheeled him over to a sitting area. Grandma sat in
the cushioned chair next to him.

"Maggie, shall we bring him in for supper later? Did the
doctor provide instructions for his meals?"

Grandma spoke with Papa and Mama at length. I gave
Grandpa a kiss on the cheek. Then I ducked out of the room
to give them privacy.

I headed upstairs to move my belongings back to my

room. Then I sat on the edge of my bed as I exhaled a long breath.

So many changes. James and I were courting. Grandpa was ailing. Grandma needed us more than ever. Mama's heart ached.

Papa's did too. I knew how close he was to Grandpa. Mama told me his own father had been harsh and unloving. It made sense to me that Grandpa filled that void for my papa. Grandpa loved and encouraged those who were around him. When I thought about men who embodied the love of Christ, Grandpa was the first to come to mind.

My emotions battled within me. I had a few exciting events to look forward to. The Independence Day Ball with James on Tuesday. The other was significantly more exciting: The World's Fair. I only needed to be patient.

The loss of Grandpa's health and empathy for Grandma took my thoughts in a sad direction. My words to Mama earlier hadn't felt like my own. I needed to hear them as much as she had. I needed to remember that I should not borrow trouble from tomorrow or the future. None of us knew when tragedy would strike. Though it tempted my mind to go there, my earlier words were right. It would steal my joy from the present.

A soft knock sounded on my door.

"Come in!"

"How are you holding up?" Papa asked as he took a seat next to me.

"Well enough. On one hand, the grief presses on my heart. On the other, I'm grateful and humbled that we can help Grandma."

"She was very pleased with how you and Mel arranged everything. Thank you for helping."

"Of course." I took my papa's hand in mine. "How are

you doing?"

Papa sighed heavily. "As well as possible. It's hard to see just how different George is. When I look into his eyes, I see he is as alert and vibrant as ever. He must be frustrated to be so... Diminished."

I nodded.

Papa rubbed his hands on his legs as he sucked in a deep breath. "Anyway, supper is ready."

He stood, and I followed him downstairs to the dining room. Clinton wheeled Grandpa to a place between Mama and Grandma. Then he took a seat next to Grandma.

Then Papa blessed the meal.

When Grandma fed Grandpa soup, much of it dribbled down his face. I bit my lip to keep the tears at bay.

"Mama, let's have the cook put it in a mug. That would be easier."

Mama stood and entered the kitchen. The cook followed her and collected the soup. Then she returned a moment later with a mug full of the soup.

"Mrs. Larson," the cook said, "let me know if you need a refill of the soup and I'll bring it right away." She disappeared into the kitchen again.

The mug seemed easier to work with. When Mama finished her meal, she offered to help Grandpa so Grandma could eat. The family barely talked as most of us watched Grandma and Grandpa figure out how to manage.

When I finished, I excused myself and went outside to the swing on the porch. I prayed for my grandparents and asked for wisdom to know how to best help them.

"Good evening."

I looked up to see James standing in front of me.

"Lost in your thoughts?"

I patted the seat next to me. As he rested his arm on my

shoulders, I snuggled into his side.

"Grandpa and Grandma are all moved in."

"How is George?"

Through sentences dotted with the occasional sob, I told him.

James rubbed my arm. "In time, everyone will settle into a new routine."

"How are things at the railway?" I asked.

His arm stiffened. "We've had to drop rates on the freight again to compete with Bullock."

I sucked in a sharp breath. "That's not good, is it?"

"No." He rubbed his other hand on the back of his neck. "We also reduced our passenger fares for Independence Day, well, the whole week really. I hope the volume of people expected makes up for it."

When I leaned my head against his shoulder, I tucked my legs to the side on the porch swing. He pushed it into a gentle motion. Then he rested his head against mine.

"Between the financial panic, these rate wars, and your grandfather's health, it feels a bit like the world is turning upside down," he whispered. "When I sit here with you, I feel like I can take on this crazy world."

"Me? What do I do?"

"For a few minutes, sitting next to you, I don't feel so alone."

My heart fluttered and filled with admiration for him. My confident, take-charge man showed his soft spot. Loneliness. I was glad to be a comfort to him.

We sat for a long time in silence. The door opened and Papa stepped onto the porch. He lit his pipe. Then he sat in a chair nearby.

"Evening, James. How long have you been out here?"

James started to slide his arm away, but I laced my fingers with his to stop him.

"Not really certain."

Papa raised an eyebrow and puffed on his pipe.

"Don't worry, Papa. He's behaved himself," I teased.

Papa blew out the smoke and laughed. "I should hope so."

"Have you had supper?" James asked.

"Yes, a while ago."

He moved his arm and stood. "I should go. I haven't eaten yet."

"Let me see if there are leftovers."

"No, that's alright." The sadness in his tone revealed his true heart.

I grabbed his hand and ushered him inside to the dining room. Then I entered the kitchen and found our cook. She gladly fixed up a plate for James and brought it into the dining room. I sat across from him.

"It seems wrong to eat in front of you while you stare at me."

"There's no better view."

He gave me a wry smile. Then he bowed his head for a minute before he started eating.

While he ate, I shared more details about Grandpa's health. Then I told him everything I read in the paper about the Independence Day celebration. When he finished, he made no move to leave. We talked for a long time about everything and nothing. I wondered if that was what marriage to him would be like. Easy conversation. Peace and joy just being in each other's presence.

Finally, around nine o'clock, Mama suggested he head home. I escorted him to the door, and he gave me a quick kiss before he left. My heart missed him already.

CHAPTER 21

JAMES

The fourth of July was a delightful distraction from the relentless pressure mounting on my shoulders.

Keri met me at the baseball field where we cheered on the Colter Cowboys. Every time Sam threw a pitch, I yelled louder. I sat in his line of sight, so he knew it was me rooting for him. I hoped it might help him forgive me if he knew I held no hard feelings.

"That was amazing!" Keri said, as the game concluded. "You didn't tell me Sam was such a good pitcher."

"Let's go congratulate him," I said as I clasped her hand and hurried over to where he stood with our family.

I released Keri's hand. Then I tugged Sam forward for a hug and pat on the back. "Great job. I knew you would win."

Boone placed an arm around both me and Sam. He squeezed the base of Sam's neck. "That curve ball really caught them off guard again this year. One of these years they'll figure it out." He released his hold on us both.

"When are you going to play again, James?" Grady asked. "We miss having you as part of the team."

"You play?" Keri asked.

"I don't have time for practice. It's been far too long since I've played."

"We could always put you way out in left field," Grady teased.

I laughed. "I doubt I'd be much help, even there."

Mama came up next to me and looped her hand over the crook of my arm. Keri walked on my other side.

"Thank you for your overt show of support," she said. "I think Sam is warming up."

"Of course, Mama."

"Preston is back in town."

I glanced at Mama.

"Sober. Changed."

"For how long?" I muttered under my breath.

"He is staying at the ranch for a few days. He's been sober the entire time."

I held back a snort. I didn't trust that he was really over his brooding. He spent many years drunk, drifting from place to place. It was hard to picture him any differently.

"He's entered the bucking bronco competition."

"And you're fine with that?" I asked.

"It's better than… Than what he's done these last few years."

"We should watch him compete," Keri suggested.

Mama relayed the details, then Keri and I meandered through the crowd on our own.

"Did your grandpa come?"

"No. He felt poorly last night, and Grandma wanted to keep him home for the day."

That afternoon, we watched Preston compete. I saw the same thing as Mama. He seemed different somehow. I hoped it lasted, though I doubted it would. We didn't stay to see the final results.

Instead, I walked Keri home late in the afternoon so she could rest for a bit before the ball. I went back to the fair for supper and sat with my family. We caught up on the news before I walked home to dress for the ball.

I decided on a navy suit and vest with a red neck scarf. Many men would opt for a navy that night, but I didn't mind. We were celebrating our nation's birthday.

While I walked toward Keri's house to pick her up, I whistled. For the first time in a long time, satisfaction and peace filled my heart.

When I entered the Glassman home, I was unprepared for the sight of Keri. My breath left in a whoosh as I took in her elegant gown. It was a navy gown with a red sash accenting her waist. She fashioned her hair into ringlets woven with a matching red ribbon. The neckline. I cleared my throat. It flattered her in ways that sent my blood pumping.

"Good evening, James." Her smile lit the entire room.

I offered my arm and eventually recovered my voice. "You look stunning."

Pink circles tinged her soft cheeks.

I led the way with her on my arm as Alex and Mel follow-ed behind.

Once we were at the ball, we kept some distance from her parents. It reminded me of the first time I noticed her. Those same sapphire eyes twinkled in the low light. I placed my hand on her waist and pulled her close. Then she clasped my other hand as we danced to a waltz.

We said little during the first few dances. My eyes never left hers. Love for her overwhelmed my heart. I wanted to marry her.

The thought caused my heart to stutter. I nearly stepped on her foot, but recovered quickly.

"Do you remember our first dance?" Keri asked.

"Yes. You captured my attention from across the room."

I spun her around and pulled her back to me.

She laughed. "At first, I believed you would veer off to some other woman. I doubted you were really interested in me."

My fingers caressed her waist where they rested. "Were there other women there? I only saw you."

Her cheeks bloomed pink as she glanced down. When her eyes connected with mine again, I saw her love for me.

"Thank you." Her voice was a whisper.

"For choosing you? It wasn't a choice. For me, there was only you."

"Oh. For that and for everything you've done over the past few weeks. Helping with my grandparents. Listening to me. Sitting with me."

I breathed deeply as I searched for the right words. "You'd do the same for me."

She smiled.

As the music finished with a flourish, I dipped her back before reeling her close again. I kissed her softly and far too quickly for my taste. I relished dancing with her.

"Would you care for some refreshments?" I asked after that dance. She nodded.

We made our way to a table and sat as we sipped punch. After a song or two, Alex and Mel found us. Alex escorted his daughter onto the dance floor.

"Mel, would you care to dance?"

"No, thank you. I'd much rather sit for a while."

After I retrieved some punch for her, I sat at the table, and I asked her, "Why do you dislike me?"

As she sipped the punch, she studied my face. Then she sighed.

140

"I don't dislike you, James. I respect you and think you are an impressive young businessman."

My eyes traveled to Keri and Alex. She smiled and laughed with her father, who she clearly adored.

"I… I'm having a hard time accepting that she is a grown woman now."

My gaze returned to Mel. She picked at some lint on the tablecloth. Then she downed the rest of her punch. As she set the cup on the table, she looked directly at me.

"I want her to be happy. I'm concerned that she still may be too young to discern true love."

I held my breath for a moment. My heart raced as her honesty troubled me.

"I know she is happy with you now. I just worry she doesn't know her heart well enough to know if she is ready for a lifetime commitment."

Mel's eyes left mine and scanned the room for her husband. "Alex thinks I'm overprotective. I know my daughter, and that concerns me." Her gaze returned to me. "I have no doubt that you love her and will treat her well."

"But you doubt her feelings for me?"

Mel straightened in her chair. "I don't doubt that her feelings are strong. Seeing you together out there has made that abundantly clear. I doubt her ability to understand what is required for a marriage."

Alex and Keri returned to the table before I could respond. Keri grabbed my hands and pulled me back out to the dance floor. The music's beat picked up, and I spent the rest of the evening dancing with the woman I intended to make my wife, despite her mother's concern.

Yet, after I walked home from dropping her off at her house, my mind chewed over Mel's words. I wondered if anyone truly understood the level of commitment needed for a strong marriage when they first made the commitment. I found it hard to believe that Mel herself would have known.

Though the conversation bothered me, I refused to let it root too deeply in my mind. If Keri loved me and I loved her, I knew that would be enough.

CHAPTER 22

JAMES

The first week of August brought additional stress. The territory assessed a larger tax on our railway. Ours was not the only one affected. Most of the railroads would pay fifteen percent more that year—a year where the industry experienced financial tightening.

I ran a hand through my hair after Jedediah Cole, our chief financial officer, left my office with the bad news. We were past due on our tax debt. It was one of several issues he raised. We were also behind on our payments to Arizona Lumber and Timber Company out of Flagstaff. Jedediah tried many times to negotiate a payment plan, but the lumber company rejected each of his proposals. They wanted our account brought current or they would pursue legal action.

"Gerard!"

My secretary entered my office. "Sir?"

"Get me the contract for Arizona Lumber."

He returned a few minutes later and handed me the documents. I flipped through them, but my brain quickly tripped over the legal terminology.

Grabbing the contract, I headed across the plaza to Keri's office. She was busy when I first arrived, so I waited in the lobby for her.

The receptionist finally took me back to her office.

"James, what brings you by this afternoon?"

I handed her the contract. "Arizona Lumber is threatening to take us to court if we don't pay in full. They refuse any type of payment plan."

"Let me look. Have a seat."

As she scanned the first few pages, I paced the room. She looked up.

"Please sit. You're making me nervous."

"Sorry."

I sank onto a chair across from her. My foot tapped a rhythm against the wood floor as my anxiety refused to settle.

"James. Would you like me to find you when I've reviewed this?"

"I'll be at the café," I said as I rushed out of her office.

While I waited, I ordered a coffee. Twenty minutes later, Keri joined me. She kissed me on the cheek before she sat across from me.

"Unfortunately, the terms of the contract are clear. They have every right to request payment in full."

I slammed my fist down on the table, which sent silverware clattering. Keri jumped.

"I'm sorry," I said through gritted teeth. The SFP&P continued to bleed money. I felt completely helpless to stop it.

"Calm down. Papa can handle the case for you if you like."

I shook my head. "I can't pay him. Our general counsel will see to it."

"Are you sure?"

I stood and tossed a few coins on the table to cover the cost of my coffee before I snatched the contract from her hands.

"I have to go." I turned and headed back to my office.

As I walked, the guilt penetrated my hard heart. I should have thanked her. I should not have been so terse. She only wanted to help. It wasn't her fault that my company inched closer and closer to the brink.

Back at the office, I relayed the news to Frank and our general counsel.

Within the week, Arizona Lumber took us to court. The judge awarded them a lien on the SFP&P. The afternoon I received the news, Frank entered my office.

"We must pick up the pace on the construction of the Granite Station and Jerome Junction. Our best hope to dig out of our financial hole is to increase our revenue by shipping the ore from the Jerome mines."

"How do you propose we pay for that?"

He grinned. "A loan from my bank."

I frowned. "Is the Prescott National Bank's board amenable?"

He nodded.

I puffed my cheeks and blew out a long breath. "Are you sure?"

"I believe in the railway. We only need funds for a few more months before things turn around. I can feel it."

Either he knew something I did not, or he suffered from gross overconfidence. Yet, he willingly put his bank on the line.

"Alright. You get us the money and I'll make it happen."

Within a few days, I traveled up to Granite Station to oversee the construction. I stayed in my private railcar and remained at the site for a week.

After the sun went down, the loneliness took over. I missed Keri. I never apologized for my curt behavior the previous week. At least I sent her a note to let her know I was out of town. Still, I owed her an apology.

I owed her more than that. I still owed her a trip to the World's Fair. A trip. With Keri. That was exactly what I needed. To get away. To stop working for a few weeks and escape the pressure.

The second day at Granite Station started early. At sunrise, I left the quiet of my private car. I walked to the construction manager's office. After strongly encouraging him to push the men harder, I watched their progress. It seemed to improve after that. Until a monsoon storm rolled in that afternoon. Then construction came to an abrupt stop.

I returned to my private car and waited the storm out. The construction manager told me it would delay them until the ground dried up.

That evening, I headed back to Prescott, and to my large, empty home.

Anger boiled. Nothing I did made a difference. My railroad was going to fail. I sensed it. The thought consumed me. No matter what. No matter how much money Frank sank into it. As long as Bullock's line remained open, it doomed both railways.

What would I be without my job? Without the railroad?

My career and business acumen became my identity. James Colter was a railroad man. Not a rancher. Not a horse trainer. A railroad magnate.

My throat constricted as my mind played out scenarios. My financial resources were plentiful. But money didn't really matter to me. Work made me who I was and drove me.

I scrounged around for my Bible and sat in the parlor

near the fireplace. I flipped through several pages, looking for what I did not know.

Then my eyes snagged on a verse in Jeremiah. *Cursed is the man who trusts in man and makes flesh his strength, whose heart turns away from the Lord. He is like a shrub in the desert, and shall not see any good come. He shall dwell in the parched places of the wilderness, in an uninhabited salt land.*

As the words sliced through my heart, I coughed. I relied on man. Frank. Myself. He and I were going to save the SFP&P, by sheer force of will. At least, that was how I acted.

No wonder I felt overwhelmed and empty. Not once did I ask God for wisdom or to help the company survive.

I snorted. Nor did I ask Him what He would have me do.

The conviction pierced my soul, though I delayed my response to it, and I continued to read.

Blessed is the man who trusts in the Lord, whose trust is the Lord. He is like a tree planted by water, that sends out its roots by the stream, and does not fear when heat comes, for its leaves remain green, and is not anxious in the year of drought, for it does not cease to bear fruit.

Does not fear when heat comes. I lived and breathed and faced the heat of the financial panic and its outcome every day. Anxiety consumed my thoughts.

With a quick snap, I closed my Bible before I set it on the end table. Then I leaned forward and propped my elbows on my knees as I closed my eyes.

I confessed my failure to trust God and admitted I tried to fix the railroad by relying on my knowledge and understanding. God wanted me to trust him with my career and company, so I surrendered my ambition to Him.

Though I hoped peace would flood me instantly, it did not. The small amount I felt gave me the determination to trust God going forward.

CHAPTER 23

KERI

A week and a half after I reviewed the lumber contract for James, he sent flowers to the office for me with a note.

"I'm sorry I took my frustration out on you. Thank you for your help. I'm finally back in Prescott and hope that you will join me for supper tonight at my home. Always yours, James."

I reread the note a few times. Then I sighed.

His curt demeanor that afternoon at the café hurt. I was glad to receive his note and the flowers, even though it took him longer to reach out than I would have liked.

Papa entered my office. "Those are lovely." He leaned over the vase and smelled the flowers. "I take it you've heard from James?"

I smiled. "He's asked me to meet him for supper." I omitted the location on purpose, as I knew Papa would not approve.

"What time can I expect you home?"

"Eight o'clock?"

Papa held my gaze. Then he slowly nodded. "Make sure he walks you home."

I stood and kissed Papa's cheek. "Don't worry so much. I'll be fine."

A short time later, Mama and Papa left the office for home. I checked my appearance and then headed out as Papa's secretary locked up.

Thankfully, James included directions in his card as I'd not visited his home before.

When I stood in front of the largest house I'd ever seen, I double checked the house number on the card with the one on the pillar of the porch. It was correct.

My heart raced. I knew he was wealthy. Yet, his home was almost twice the size of my family home. I squared my shoulders and straightened my back before I knocked.

An awkward amount of time passed before James greeted me.

"Sorry. I was in the back."

He held the door wide, and I stared at the crystal chandelier in the entryway. It reminded me of the ostentatious one in the dining room of the Palmer House in Chicago.

As I moved past him, he rested his hand on the small of my back. I bit the inside of my lip to keep my jaw from gaping over the opulence of his home.

"Do you like it?"

I turned to face him. His eyes looked hopeful.

"It's beautiful."

A grin stretched across his lips. "This way."

When we entered the dining room, my breath caught. The light reflected off the polished surface of the dark cherry wood table. Candles on the table set the mood, along with a lovely floral centerpiece that matched the bouquet he sent to my office. Two place settings sat across from each other at the far end of the table. He led me to the chair in front of one of them. I sat, then he took the seat across from me.

"First, before we eat, I'd like to apologize again. I treated you poorly when you helped me with the contract. I'm sorry for that."

I smiled. "I forgive you."

"Thank you."

He rang a small silver bell. A middle-aged Mexican woman entered the room and laid out the meal. "Thank you, Maria."

She smiled at me and left.

James reached across the table for my hands. I gently clasped his as he prayed over the meal. Once he finished, he served me before he served himself.

"This is delicious." I swallowed the first bite of the roast chicken.

"Maria is a fine cook and housekeeper."

A few minutes of silence passed. Then James slid an envelope across the table toward me.

"A gift for you."

I set down my silverware and opened it. Train tickets. I quirked an eyebrow.

"Read the destination."

I glanced down. Then I squealed. "Chicago? Are you taking me to the World's Fair?"

"Yes, my love. I'm keeping my promise. We leave in two weeks."

I stood and scurried around the table. Then I planted a big kiss on his cheek as I hugged him. "Thank you."

He chuckled. "You're more excited than I expected."

After I took my seat again, I asked, "How long will we be gone?"

"A month."

My breath caught. "Can you take that much time off?"

He sighed heavily. "Frank agreed that I'm overdue for time off. There's no need for both of us to be hands-on right now. When we start construction on the southern part of the line again, then he'll need me."

"A month," I whispered.

"Shall I speak to your father?"

I shook my head. Papa would insist on a chaperone, and I wanted James all to myself. No sharp overprotective eyes scowling at me everywhere I went. "I'll speak to him."

When we finished our meal, James rang the silver bell. Maria took our dishes and silverware away. A few minutes later, she brought out a piece of chocolate cake for each of us.

I closed my eyes as I took a bite. "Decadent."

He laughed. "You love savoring your meal, don't you?"

"Of course. Especially a dessert like this. We never have chocolate cake."

"If you are one day the lady of this house, you can decide what we have for dessert."

My heart pounded against my rib cage. It was the first time he sounded serious about marriage.

"Would you like that?" he asked as his smile faded.

"Deciding what we have for dessert or being your wife?" The last word left my lips in a whisper.

"Both."

"Yes."

"Good. I thought you might." His eyes belied his teasing tone.

My heart fluttered. Somehow, I finished the chocolate cake.

"How are your grandparents?"

I blinked as my mind struggled to switch to the new topic. I took a deep breath before I answered.

"They have settled into a routine. Grandpa gets stronger every day. The doctor encourages us to help him walk a little more each day. He also gave Grandpa some exercises to help strengthen his right arm again."

"I'm glad to hear it. Do you think he'll be able to attend church soon?"

I shook my head. "Not for some time yet."

James escorted me into the parlor as I continued. "Papa had a ramp built on the porch last week so we can walk with Grandpa in his wheeled chair. Grandma loves to stroll with him after the heat of the day lifts."

The clock on the mantle struck eight.

"Oh, my goodness. I promised Papa I would be home by eight o'clock."

James stood and accompanied me home. Papa waited on the porch for me, so James gave me a kiss on the cheek.

"I look forward to our trip," he whispered. "Let me know what exhibits you want to see. If any require advance purchase, I'll pay."

"Thank you, again, James."

I watched as he walked down the street. My heart warmed as my anticipation rose. I could barely wait for two weeks to go by.

A few days later, I told Mama and Papa about the trip. Mama was not pleased.

"You are only courting."

I took a deep breath as the lie formed in my mind. "A chaperone will be present the entire time. There's no reason to worry."

Papa studied me for a solid minute. Just when I thought he would not agree, he spoke.

"You may go."

"Alex—"

"Mel, she wants to go. She has a chaperone. Neither you nor I can go with her. So what harm is there?"

Mama frowned. She crossed her arms over her chest and locked her gaze with mine. I saw disappointment in her eyes. As far as she knew, I did nothing to warrant the look. At length, she finally consented. "Fine."

After I hugged them both, I ascended the stairs. A brief stab of guilt pricked my heart for lying to them. As their voices carried, I slowed my steps.

"I don't trust her," Mama said. "I have a bad feeling about this."

"She's a grown woman. Forbidding her to go will only drive her to go behind our backs. We've talked about this before."

I paused at the top of the stairs, out of sight.

"If she makes a mistake, she will live with the consequences of it," Papa said. "In the meantime, if you are worried, pray."

Their voices grew softer, so I retired to my room. I did not understand Mama. I knew how she and Papa met. They married in less than two months after meeting. Grandpa married Grandma in a few short months of meeting. James and I started courting four months ago, which sounded like a long time compared to both relationships.

James insinuated he wanted to marry me. I already knew my answer. Whenever he asked, it would be a warm heartfelt "Yes" with no reservation. I wished Mama understood that.

Regardless, James and I would visit the World's Fair without the scrutiny of judging eyes. I would show Mama that I could make my own decisions and watch out for myself.

CHAPTER 24

JAMES

The first Monday of September finally arrived. I rented a carriage and picked up Keri from her home early that morning as my excitement rose. Her father loaded her trunks in the carriage, then helped her up.

"Be safe," he said.

"Papa, I'll be fine. I love you."

Alex nodded as he coughed. Mel stood in the porch's shadow. Her expression looked like she thought I was about to murder her daughter, not take her on a coveted trip.

I sighed and slapped the reins on the horse.

Keri waved to her parents as we drove down the street. Within minutes, I pulled the carriage to a stop in front of the train station. The porter loaded our trunks on a cart and took them to the baggage car. A young man offered to return our horse and carriage to the livery. I tipped him with a few coins.

Then I offered Keri my arm and led her to the train. We took our seats. Twenty minutes later, the train left the station.

I patted my vest pocket. The ring was still there. During

the trip, I planned to ask her to be my wife. I had not decided the precise timing, other than I would before we returned to Prescott. I hoped some sight or exhibit at the fair would provide the perfect romantic setting.

I cleared my throat. "I can't believe your parents agreed to let you come unchaperoned."

Keri smiled at me and held my gaze. "Believe it."

When her eyes darted away quickly, I held back a frown and wondered if she just lied to me. I wasn't about to send her back home, so I pushed away my concern and reached for my book. The trip to Chicago would take three days, which gave me plenty of time to read. I couldn't remember the last time I read something other than the newspaper. As I opened the book, Keri leaned against my arm. I looped it around her shoulder, and she nestled against me. By the time we reached Rock Butte, she fell asleep.

———

We arrived in Chicago on Thursday, September 7th without incident. I hailed a carriage. The young man loaded our trunks in the back, and we climbed inside.

"Congress Plaza Hotel," I said.

"I can't believe we're really here." Keri's eyes lit with excitement.

I took her hand and laced my fingers with hers. My broad smile matched hers.

When the carriage slowed, the doorman of the hotel held the carriage door open and helped Keri down. I followed her. We both looked up to take in the tall eleven-story building. The outside was rather plain compared to the Palmer House, where I usually stayed.

We entered the lobby.

"Oh, my!" Keri exclaimed.

The marbled floor beckoned us forward. Ornate Victorian chairs and sofas sat in groupings throughout the lobby. Gilded sconces with a dozen candles each lit the way. Each squared pillar flanking the room held the sconces on each side. They painted the transom ceiling with scenic frescoes, which reminded me of the Palmer House's dining room.

I escorted Keri to the front desk.

"Colter."

"Good afternoon, Mr. & Mrs. Colter."

I coughed. Keri's eyes went wide. "Pardon?"

"We have the honeymoon suite ready for you."

Keri frowned. "James—"

"Take a seat," I asked her, "while I sort this out. I most certainly did not reserve the honeymoon suite."

Once Keri sat down, I spoke to the clerk. "Mr. James Colter. I should have two adjacent rooms, not the honeymoon suite."

The clerk frowned. "Yes, Mr. James Colter from Arizona, correct?"

"Yes."

He ran his finger down the ledger and pointed to the room name. "Honeymoon suite."

I growled. Gerard. I would have words with my secretary when I returned, that was if I didn't fire him.

"Do you have two rooms available?"

"I'm sorry sir, we are full. With the Columbian Exposition, we won't have anything open until later this month."

"Not even one room?"

The clerk shook his head.

"Give me the keys."

"I'm sorry for the inconvenience. Please," he handed me two cards, "have supper on us this evening."

I took the cards and keys from the clerk's hand as my stomach dropped. Once I saw the room, I would decide if alternate arrangements were required.

"Keri," I said as I offered her my arm. "Please know that I asked for two separate adjacent rooms. Unfortunately, Gerard booked us the honeymoon suite and there are no other rooms available."

Keri bit her lower lip as we entered the elevator. The operator stopped on the eleventh floor.

"We'll see what it is like. If you're not comfortable, then I will stay somewhere else."

The elevator operator snorted.

"Got something to say?"

"Sorry, sir. I doubt you will find anything at this late date." He opened the gates on the elevator and motioned for us to exit.

I took Keri's hand in mine and steered her down the hall to room 1106. I turned the key and pushed the door open.

"Oh, my!" she exclaimed as she dropped her hold on my arm.

The suite was massive, with a spectacular view of the lake. Gold glittered everywhere: the paint, the lighting, and the fixtures on the wet bar. They arranged the chairs and sofas in front of an enormous marble fireplace. Its fire glowed and cast dancing shadows on the marble. The curtains were purple velvet with gold fleur-de-lis designs. They complimented the floral design on the furniture.

Keri stood in front of one of the floor-to-ceiling windows. "It's beautiful."

I moved to stand behind her. Then I wrapped my arms around her. "I'm sorry for the mistake with the room."

She craned her neck to look at me. "Don't be. I think we can make this work."

I leaned my head down to trail kisses along her neck. She sighed, then turned to face me. My lips captured hers as she wrapped her arms around my middle and pressed close. I deepened the kiss until a noise behind me shook me back to reality.

"Sorry, sir," the bellman announced his presence. "The door was open."

I released my hold on Keri and crossed the room.

"Where would you like your things?"

Keri answered before I could. "In the bedroom."

My heart raced. I started to object, but she placed a hand on my arm. When the bellman finished, he held out his hand, and I pressed a few coins into it. Then I locked the door behind him.

Keri explored the bedroom as I sank onto a chair by the ornately carved dark wood table. A bottle of champagne rested in a bucket of ice. A plate of chocolate-dipped strawberries was next to it.

I snorted. Honeymoon suite. Everything about the room invoked romantic feelings in me. It was not good. I couldn't stay there.

Not unless I married her.

Some of the heaviness lifted from my shoulders. Perhaps that was the solution. I could propose tonight, and we could marry in the morning. Then the trip would be our honeymoon.

Keri stood in the bedroom's doorway. The light behind her made her silhouette glow. My lips turned up on one side.

"Come," I said as I held out one hand.

When she crossed the room and took my hand, I dropped to one knee and dug in my vest pocket for the ring.

CHAPTER 25

KERI

When James dropped to his knee, my breath left my lungs. It was the perfect setting. It almost made me wonder if that had been his plan all along.

"Keri, you know I love you. You are smart, beautiful, kind. When I am apart from you, you are never far from my thoughts. When I first danced with you two years ago, we shared a connection, one that has blossomed and grown since we started courting this year. I cannot imagine my life without you, and I want you to be my wife. I want to spend the rest of my life with you by my side. Will you marry me?"

I took a deep breath and smiled. "Yes. Of course."

Then he drew me into his arms and lavished me with kisses as he slid the ring onto my finger. His hands pressed me close, before I could study the ring. Fire traveled from my heart to my toes and back again as I returned his kisses. After several minutes, he slowed the kiss and ended it. He rested his forehead on mine as I tried to catch my breath.

"How would you feel about getting married tomorrow, at the exposition?"

"I would love to." Then I pushed away from him. "That would certainly solve the problem of our accommodations."

The look in his eyes intensified, causing my heart to throb. He cleared his throat.

"I'll be right back." He left the room.

After I entered the bedroom, I unpacked my trunks. I hung my dresses in the wardrobe and studied each one. The ivory and gold silk dress that I brought would make a lovely wedding gown. I set my hair pins, brush, and face powder on the vanity.

While James was gone, I changed into a pale blue evening gown. Then I splashed some water on my face and patted it dry before I applied more face powder. I unpinned my hair and brushed it out. Then I fashioned it high on my head, with long ringlets cascading down my back. I smiled, pleased with my appearance.

As I stepped from the bedroom, James returned. He coughed.

"You look gorgeous." His voice was husky. "Have a seat while I freshen up. Then we'll go down for supper."

I nodded, though I did not sit. Instead, I walked around the large room of the suite. Everything about the room sparkled and glittered in the light. It stirred warm feelings.

I snagged one of the chocolate-covered strawberries from the plate and bit into it as James emerged from the bedroom.

He groaned. "Tonight is going to be torture with you looking like that."

I swallowed the strawberry. "Perhaps we should head down to the dining room."

He offered his arm and escorted me to the elevator. The operator was waiting for us. I wondered if there was always one waiting for the top floor.

Within minutes, we entered the palatial dining room. In some ways, it reminded me of the dining room of the Palmer House. Painted frescoes covered the transom ceiling. Instead of the dark wood ensconced pillars of the Palmer House, the Congress Plaza's pillars were bright yellow with flecks of gold. The sconces matched the elaborate arrangements in the lobby.

The maître d' showed us to a secluded table with a view of the lake. He lit the candles on the table. The soft glow reflected in James's eyes.

My heart fluttered. Tomorrow I would be his wife. I glanced down at the ring. The grand diamond glistened in the soft light.

"Do you have wedding bands already?"

He winked at me. "I will by tomorrow morning."

I laughed. "Was this all part of your plan?"

He shook his head. "Not exactly. I knew I would propose sometime on this trip. The mix up with the room sped up my plan."

He reached for my hand. "If this is too fast, we can wait. I don't want you to feel pressured."

I lowered my lashes, then looked up into his deep brown eyes. "I want to marry you. Tomorrow. Tonight, if I could."

He let out a shaky breath. "Don't tempt me."

"What is the plan for tomorrow, then?"

"It took some doing. The concierge bribed the wedding chapel at the fair to put us at the front of the list. I won't tell you how much that set me back." He winked at me. "So, at nine o'clock, we will stand before a minister and say our vows."

My smile grew wider. It was really happening. I was about to become Mrs. James Colter.

"The rest of the day is up to you." He wiggled his eyebrows. "I know how I'd like to spend the day, but I will defer to my wife."

"Hmm. A lazy day in the honeymoon suite sounds lovely. Perhaps we could go to the fair in the evening and see the electricity lights or go on a gondola ride?"

The server set our meal in front of us. When he left, James finally responded, "That sounds perfect to me."

After he blessed the meal, I blurted out one of the many questions tugging my heart. "James, are you nervous about being a father?"

His eyes softened. "Not at all. I've enjoyed being an uncle to Boone's son. Every time I see him, I look forward to the day when I'll hold my son."

"Or daughter?"

He smiled. "Or daughter."

"I'm worried I won't be a good mother." I looked out the window and watched boats float toward the dock on the lake.

"Keri. Look at me."

I did.

"I saw how you were with Amelia when your grandpa was ill. You are a natural mother. I am confident you will be a good one to our children."

My pulse raced as I wondered if children might come along sooner than I hoped. I expected to have time to establish my career before becoming a mother. Yet, if I married James tomorrow, our lazy afternoon at the hotel could certainly lead to children. My cheeks warmed.

"I know we haven't talked about this before. Would you mind if I work at the law office? Or the railroad, if things turn around?"

He cleared his throat as I took a bite of my meal.

"I know it is important to you. If your concern is financial, know that I can provide for you. Even if," his eyes darted away, "the railroad goes under. I have plenty saved. More than enough until I find other work."

"I'm not concerned about the money. It's the work itself. You saw firsthand how gifted I am. I'd like to keep working, especially if I could come back to the SFP&P."

As I waited for him to respond, I took a sip of water.

"When children come, if you want to keep working, then we'll hire whatever help you deem necessary."

I smiled. "Thank you, James."

He smiled. "Anything for you, my love."

———

The next morning, he knocked on the door to wake me. I wore a robe so he could retrieve his things before he dressed in the main room. I closed the door behind him and pulled the ivory and gold dress from the wardrobe. Even though I commissioned the dress specifically for our trip, I didn't know it would become my wedding dress. I washed up and donned the lovely gown before I brushed my hair. My hands shook with excitement. We were getting married in just a few hours.

My hair took more time than I expected. I wished Mama was there to help. She wasn't and a brief pang of guilt niggled at my heart. I shook it off and finished pinning my hair in place. Then I stood and opened the door.

When I found James sitting at the table, he stood. His throat worked and his eyes spoke of love and desire. He crossed the room and held up my fur coat before he gently settled it into place. Then he offered me his arm.

"Shall we go?" His voice was husky.

I managed a nod.

In the hallway, he said, "You look more lovely than ever. That dress." He took a deep breath. "If I didn't know better, I'd say it's truly a wedding dress."

"You look rather dashing yourself." I gave him a coy smile.

He looked incredibly handsome in his black suit. He wore a gold vest and a neck scarf. His black top hat and dark wood walking stick completed the sophisticated look.

"If I didn't know better," I teased, "I would think you intended your suit for our wedding day."

He laughed, and little lines formed by his intense eyes. "I brought it for when I planned to propose, so you were close."

Once we exited the elevator, he led me to the carriage waiting outside. The chilly morning air bit through my dress and I pulled my coat closed.

The ride to the fairgrounds took roughly fifteen minutes. The carriage driver continued through the entrance and down a cobblestone path until we stopped in front of a chapel. A footman helped me down. Then he showed us into the simple chapel.

A pastor stood in front of the altar.

"Mr. Colter?"

James shook his hand and introduced us.

"Do you have rings?"

James pulled them from his pocket and handed them to the pastor. Then he turned and faced me. He held my hands in his as I gazed into his eyes.

I smiled as I repeated the vows. His hands shook as he repeated his vows to me. Then we exchanged rings.

The pastor announced we were husband and wife. "You may kiss your bride."

James pulled me close and dipped me back for a barely restrained kiss. When he ended the kiss, I breathed heavily and smiled.

The pastor asked us to sign the marriage license. Then he handed it to James.

My husband. James whisked me back to the hotel.

CHAPTER 26

World's Fair, Chicago
September 8, 1893

JAMES

My wedding was the happiest day of my life even though we eloped. I knew Mama would give me no end of grief for it. Keri's family would too.

None of that mattered to me as I stood before the pastor at the wedding chapel and promised myself to my wife. Her sapphire eyes dazzled my heart as she promised herself to me. As soon as we signed the license and I placed it in my jacket pocket, I escorted her back to the carriage and then to the hotel.

Once we were in the privacy of our honeymoon suite, I studied my wife. Most of her long brown hair piled on top of her head in a stunning arrangement, as several long ringlets cascaded down her slender back. That dress took my breath away. It accentuated her perfect figure. And I only thought about getting it off her.

I cleared my throat. "We should sit for some photos when we return to Prescott. I'm sorry I did not think of it sooner."

I stalled. I knew exactly how I wanted the next few minutes to unfold. Yet, I did not want to pressure her for intimacy. My mind and heart warred.

Until she took my hand and led me into the bedroom. Then I treated her like the princess she was and made her my wife.

———

The rest of our wedding day blurred. We talked, kissed, and whispered words of love to each other.

I thought I loved her before that day. But, on that day, my love for my wife increased tenfold.

As the afternoon wore on, I reluctantly pulled myself away from her side.

"Let's find some food and go to the fair," I suggested as I dressed in one of my more casual suits.

She laughed. "Hungry?"

"Famished. Plus," I looked over my shoulder as she threw back the covers and stood. "I promised my wife a gondola ride."

I left the bedroom and closed the door behind me. I picked up my book and smiled while I pretended to read.

In a few minutes, she joined me. She wore a high collared light blue dress; one I'd seen her wear to work before. Though the dress was simple, she looked beautiful to me.

"Mrs. Colter," I teased as I brushed a swift kiss across her lips. "Would you like to eat at the fair or before we leave?"

"I can wait until we are at the fairgrounds." She lowered her gaze, then brought it back up to me, which caused my heart to beat twice as fast. "Can you?"

I groaned. It took everything within me to leave that

room. I nudged her toward the door. "Woman, go."

I found the key and locked the door behind us.

Then we explored the food offerings at the fair. We made our way to the Italy section of the park. As we walked past a restaurant, the smells made my mouth water.

"Let's eat there."

Keri agreed, and we entered the restaurant. The server led us to a table with a view of the canal. When he handed us the menu, I studied it.

Keri looked up. "I don't know what this is. Ravioli? Ricotta?"

I smiled. "Neither do I."

When the waiter returned, we asked for his advice. He suggested the ravioli in cream sauce for Keri and a shrimp dish for me. We went with his recommendations. I also ordered a bottle of red wine.

Before our meals arrived, the server brought bread and a bottle of a greenish-gold colored oil. He drizzled some of it onto a plate. "For the bread."

I shrugged after he left. Keri ripped off a corner of bread and dabbed it in the oil.

"Oh, this is good. Try some."

She dipped another piece in oil and held it out to me. I took it and popped it in my mouth. "Not bad. Though quite different from Mama's creamy butter."

She smiled and sipped the wine. My eyes remained glued to hers throughout the meal. She shared some of her ravioli. I shared the shrimp dish. I liked her ravioli better. The fluffy filling tasted salty and cheesy.

The server brought a dessert. He called it tiramisu. When it arrived, I sliced off a bite with my fork. Then I held it up for Keri.

She giggled. "You do like feeding me, don't you?"

I nodded and smiled.

She savored the bite and finally announced her assessment. "I taste coffee and vanilla. Maybe cinnamon. I think you'll like it."

Keri took her fork and portioned a piece for me. I ate it. "I like it."

She laughed. "That's it? You like it. Nothing more?"

I shrugged. "It's good. It's a dessert. What more is there?"

We lingered at the table as the sun dipped low in the sky. Then I paid for the meal, and we headed toward the boathouse for the gondola rides.

I handed the clerk extra coins to make sure we were alone in the boat and that the gondolier would take us on the longest, most romantic ride. I stepped down into the boat and held my hand out to Keri. When she took a step, the boat shifted, and I collided with her. She made it onto the seat, though I ended up on the edge. Her laughter sounded light and free.

Before the gondolier pushed away from the dock, I sat next to my wife. I placed my arm around her shoulders and slid her close.

As the sun set and darkness fell, the water glistened with the reflection of the electricity lights.

"Oh!" Keri whispered. "The electricity lights. It's so beaut-iful."

"I've seen nothing like it before," I agreed.

The gondolier rowed us to the center of the canal, away from other boats. Then he directed the boat near a large waterfall fountain. The sound soothed my soul. There was nowhere else I wanted to be. All thoughts of the railroad vanished. It was me, Keri, and the beauty of the scene before us.

She was really my wife. Mine for life. My heart warmed

as I turned to take in her beauty. I swallowed the lump in my throat. I loved her so much.

The smile on her face filled her eyes as she absorbed the peacefulness of our surroundings. The soft glow of the lights along the bank cast gold tones on her skin.

"I love you," I whispered.

Her gaze connected with mine. Then she tilted her head, and I lowered my lips to her full lips. I kissed my wife softly, sweetly. Then I broke the contact and caressed the back of her neck while we watched the gilded buildings slowly float by.

The magical ride ended, and we walked along the bank of the canal until we grew tired. I led her to an area with carriages to take us back to our hotel.

My heart picked up pace as I unlocked the door. It still didn't seem fully real to me she was my wife. Even when we entered the bedroom and readied for sleep. As I laid next to her, I looped my arm around her and held her close. I could get used to that.

CHAPTER 27

KERI

The first few days after our wedding, we spent the afternoon and evenings at the fair. Since it was so close to our hotel, we decided for the rest of the time to spend the morning and early afternoon exploring. Then we rested at the hotel. Sometimes, I took a nap. Sometimes, James wouldn't let me. In the evenings, we returned to the fair for supper and to watch the lights.

Midway through our trip, we spent the day at the transportation building. James looked like a little boy as we me-and-ered through the exhibits.

"Motorized carriages!" he exclaimed. "I've never seen such a thing."

He tossed the exhibitor a few extra coins, so he let us sit in the motorized carriage. He showed James how it worked.

"Keri, this is fascinating."

I smiled. I found it as interesting as he did.

"One day," the exhibitor said, "these will replace the horse and buggy. Just you wait."

"Maybe this will be your next venture," I said. "When you tire of the railroad."

He laughed. "It might be just the thing. Except, I'm far from being tired of the railroad."

His smile faded. "This is the first time I've even thought about work."

He exited the motorized car before he helped me. Then he placed my hand in the crook of his arm.

"Besides marrying you," he said, "the break from work has been good for me. I needed it. Though I'll be glad to go back soon."

Part of me never wanted to leave the fair. So many fresh sights and sounds. So many new inventions. Adventure lurked around every corner. I thought life at home might seem boring after that.

The next exhibit was full of railroad locomotives from around the world. James's face brightened again as he weaved his way between the machines.

"Look at this, Keri. It's a French steam engine." He studied the details. "It's so compact compared to our engines."

He grabbed my hand. "And these are Belgian. Great for mountainous terrain."

I laughed as he tugged me toward the Empire State Express exhibit. "Engine 999. I read about this. It reaches speeds up to one hundred twelve miles an hour. We'd be in Ash Fork from Prescott in a third of the time."

He reached out and touched the smooth metal of the engine. I never tired of his child-like awe of machinery. He was so adorable.

"That one looks old," I said as I pointed to one standing nearby.

"John Bull! Let's go see it. It's a famous train. It first started service in 1831. Can you believe it? It is over sixty years old."

"I hope I look that good at sixty," I teased.

He snorted. "Me too."

I laughed. "I suppose I deserved that."

He ignored my comment as he ushered me toward it.

We spent the entire day in the transportation building. My feet hurt, so I periodically rested when I found a bench. One such time, James wandered off for thirty minutes. When he returned, he had a red and white box in his hand.

He took a handful and held his fist out. "Give me your hand."

I held my hand with my palm open. He dropped the treat in it.

"Try it."

I tossed one piece of the caramel covered popcorn in my mouth. "This is good. What is it?"

"Cracker Jacks."

I shoved the rest into my mouth. "I wonder if we could order some of this. It would be a great snack for the train ride."

James's eyes lit with excitement. "You may be on to some-thing there."

———

Our magical trip was at an end. As I packed my last dress in my trunk, reality set in. I lied to my parents and my husband about having a chaperone. I married James without my parents' permission.

I rubbed a hand over my stomach as it knotted tightly.

"Is everything alright?" James asked as he stood and moved closer.

"I'm fine." Another lie.

The bellman took our things and promised to deliver them to the train station. I grabbed my reticule. James grasped his satchel and offered me his arm. For the last time, we took the elevator down to the lobby.

"What is it? I can tell something is bothering you."

I tried to laugh his concern away. "I've had such a wonderful time and will miss it."

He smiled and patted my hand. "Truly, this has been the best month of my life. Marrying you. Getting to know you better as we saw the most amazing things at the fair."

He placed an arm around my shoulders and squeezed. Then he released me and returned the keys to the front desk. He took my hand and led me out to a waiting carriage.

"I love you," I whispered as I snuggled close to him in the carriage against the chilly fall air.

"I love you, too, Mrs. Colter." His eyes echoed his words.

Once we were on the train, my anxiety returned. I had three days left to figure out how to tell my parents and grandparents that I married James. I could already hear both Mama and Papa's arguments. Why didn't we wait to marry so the family could be present? Where was the chaperone whose job it was to prevent such a situation? What happened that required we marry in a rush?

I wrung my hands together as I stared out the window. The landscape turned flat as we entered the prairies. Only grass and brush as far as the eye could see.

One thing was certain, the issue with the room would remain my secret. I might tell them we stayed in the honeymoon suite after we married, but not before. I believed James asked for two adjoining rooms. He was too upset about it every time we discussed it.

When it was time for supper the first night on the ride home, James led me to the dining car. I ordered a sandwich, but my stomach only knotted tighter.

I pushed my sandwich away, untouched, and James noticed.

"Something is on your mind. You've been shifty and you are not eating. Talk to me, Keri."

He reached out and grabbed my hand.

"Tell me."

My gaze drifted to the bartender at the other end of the dining car. He was a stout man with thinning hair and a bushy mustache. He smiled, and I glanced back at James.

"Do you regret marrying me?" he asked as he stiffened and withdrew his hand.

"No, that's not it. I'm proud to be your wife. I love you." As I reached for his hand, I smiled. He relaxed in his chair then.

"I suppose I will need to pack when I get home."

He smiled softly. "I want my wife to live in the same house as me." He winked.

"Of course." A tightness settled into my chest, and I looked away again.

"Are you worried about your grandpa? I'm sure your parents would have sent word if anything happened. I let them know where we were staying before we left."

My eyes snapped back to his. "You did?"

"Of course. I was taking their daughter away for a month. I figured it would ease your mother's anxiety if she knew how to reach us."

I blew out a long breath. "I see."

James rubbed his thumb over the knuckles on my hand. "Please eat. It's a long trip. I wouldn't want you to starve yourself."

I withdrew my hand and forced myself to eat a few bites under his scrutiny. As I swallowed, my stomach did not revolt, but it did not feel any better either.

CHAPTER 28

JAMES

On the second morning of our train ride home, my excitement grew. We would arrive in Prescott late afternoon on Sunday. We would go home to our house together. I smiled at the thought.

Then on Monday, I would take her to her parents' house and move her things to our home. I wondered if Boone might be in town and could help.

"How much stuff do you have at your parents' house?" I asked.

She stiffened. I held back a frown. She seemed anxious from the moment we left the hotel. Something was wrong.

She cleared her throat. "Mostly clothing. A lot of dresses and hats. Some shoes. A few books. A handful of framed photographs."

"Will it fit in some trunks, or should I see if I can find some crates?"

"I… I don't know."

Her voice felt as distant as her heart. My heart squeezed tight. Something clearly bothered her, but every time I asked her, she remained tight-lipped.

"My parents are going to be livid."

Ah, at last I received the answer. "I will tell them. When we arrive at the train station, I'll take you home and I will tell them."

She turned her blue eyes on me and frowned. "And what will you tell them? That we had only one room? That we married quickly without seeking Papa's permission? I've turned this over and over in my mind for the better part of two days, James. They won't be happy, and I don't know how to make them happy."

I took her hands in mine. "I will speak to them. If you'd like, I can speak to them alone in the dining room. If they are angry, they can be angry with me and not you."

She withdrew her hands from mine. "I'm more worried about their disappointment."

She crossed her arms over her chest. "Perhaps if you give me a few days with them—"

"Absolutely not. You are my wife. Your place is in my home. Our home."

"But if I could warm them up to the idea. Tell them stories about the fair and how we enjoyed each other's company. I could soften the blow. Maybe they would be less angry with us."

My heart sliced in two. My wife was asking me if she could go home to her parents and deceive them even more instead of coming home with me. I looked away as my heart cracked. How could she suggest such a thing?

"I'm going to the club car," I said as I stood and left her.

Perhaps I had pushed her into marriage sooner than she was ready. Her mother's words came back to me. She thought Keri would not fully understand what it took for a lifetime commitment. I wondered if our present argument was exactly what Mel thought might happen.

Or was it something else entirely?

"Brandy." I ordered my drink of choice. When it arrived, I swirled it around in the glass and sipped it slowly as my mind tried to resolve my problems.

She was right about one thing: I had not asked Alex for his permission to marry his daughter. Maybe that was more important to her or him than I realized. And we did not have a wedding in front of her family. Instead, we had our wedding at a once-in-a-lifetime setting. Very few couples could claim a wedding at the Columbian Exposition.

Lifting the glass to my lips, I took another sip. The warm liquid did little to calm my anxiety.

Before that conversation with my wife, I was looking forward to returning home. I was excited to welcome her into my home, our home. I'd clear out space in the closet for her things or buy a wardrobe. For the rest of our lives, I pictured waking up next to her. I wanted her to put her touches on the home to make it ours.

Yesterday, I anticipated returning to work. My gut told me things improved at the railroad and Frank's plan worked.

Instead of excitement, anxiety overwhelmed me. I needed to figure out the best way to help my wife feel comfortable leaving her family. I had to tell her parents and grandparents I was taking her away from them. In Chicago, it never occurred to me they would see our elopement that way.

Over the next day, Keri and I politely argued. I presented her with the opportunity to let the burden fall on me. I reiterated my desire to have her move into our house immediately.

She continued to push back. I saw how her skills as an attorney could be detrimental to our marriage. She would not let her idea go.

In the end, she wore me down. I agreed to give her until Wednesday evening. After work, I would collect my wife. We agreed she would tell her family before I came to pick her up. If she failed to do so, I would tell them that evening and move her out that night. She'd be packed and ready to go.

On Sunday, just outside of Prescott, she tried to hand me the rings.

"You keep them. I would prefer if they remained on your finger, but if you feel inclined to take them off—" I coughed to hide the pain that the words caused me, "then it is your problem to figure out what to do with them."

"Fine," she replied tersely.

When we arrived at the train station, her father waited for us. There was no opportunity to give my wife a proper goodbye. Instead, I paid a man to deliver my trunks to my residence. Then I walked home dejected without my wife and without my heart, for she gripped it firmly.

———

When I arrived at work the next morning, I was unprepared for the state of affairs. Frank asked me to meet in his office first thing.

He smiled and greeted me with a warm handshake. Then he pointed to my hand. "What's this? A ring? Tell me you didn't."

I forced a brighter smile than my heart felt. "I did indeed marry Keri."

"Congratulations! I suppose your vacation turned into a honeymoon, then?"

My cheeks warmed. "It did. Enough about the loss of my bachelorhood," I teased. "Tell me the news."

"First, Robinson resigned first thing this morning. I'm currently the acting President, but he thinks the board will take his recommendation to give me the position permanently."

"Congratulations! That is excellent news."

"As soon as it is official, I'm promoting you to Vice President of Operations, my old position."

My excitement grew. "Thank you, Frank."

"You've earned it. Also, I have deposited your back pay for the months where you drew no salary."

My pulse raced. "Can we afford that?"

"Yes. We've secured several new investors from the east. They've seen how we stayed afloat during a time when other railroads failed. Investors see railroads as an excellent investment but are more discerning now. Our railroad has a fine reputation."

I let out a long breath. My railroad survived. I was getting promoted and paid. If only I could get my wife to live with me.

"You need to start construction on the southern route again. We've hired a new construction manager, but he could use some guidance, at least for the first few weeks, until he learns the job."

My throat constricted. I needed a few days to get my personal affairs in order. "When did you want me down there?"

"By Wednesday. Send the survey crew down there, too."

"Wednesday?" I hesitated.

Frank frowned. "Is that a problem?"

"No. I'll leave on Wednesday."

I left the large stack of memos and letters unread on my desk. Then I headed over to Boone's office. Both he and

Jaclyn were in.

"We need you down on the southern route. Can you be there by Wednesday?" I asked.

"Is the railway financially stable?" Boone asked. I read the concern on his face. "We don't work for free, you know."

"I'm not asking you to. If you want to raise your rate, we will cover it. We need both crews if you can spare them. We are going to finish the line to Wickenburg as soon as possible. It may take a few months, but we'll keep going until it's done."

"Alright," Boone agreed. "We'll head out Wednesday. I assume you want the crews on different parts of the construction."

"Yes. Head down to Congress and we'll flesh out where we need the teams."

I turned to leave, but Jaclyn stopped me.

"What is on your finger?" she asked.

"My wedding band."

I opened the door and walked out as I heard her ask, "Did he marry Keri?"

At that moment, I hoped the news would spread quickly. Perhaps it would motivate my wife to tell her parents and move into our home as soon as possible.

With that thought, I headed to her office. She just finished with a client, so I stole her away for an hour. We went to the bank, and I added her to my account.

"You'll need to manage the funds at home while I'm away," I told her.

"Away?"

"I'll be gone for a few weeks to the construction site starting Wednesday. I need to train the new construction manager."

"Oh, so I'm not moving on Wednesday?"

I frowned. "I would like you to stick with our plan. You should still move into our house on Wednesday. I'll make sure Maria has everything ready for you. She can also arrange for someone to pick up your things and move them in. She will continue to cook and clean for us both. But you will need to leave her the funds to purchase food and for her wage. The books are in my desk drawer in the office at home. It is unlocked."

"Alright." Her impassive tone bothered me.

"I will write to you often." Then I touched her cheek. "I love you and it would bring me peace to know you are waiting for me in our home. In a few weeks, we'll be together again, and I look forward to it."

She smiled and placed a kiss on my cheek. "I will miss you," she whispered.

I walked her back to her office and promised again to write to her often. I couldn't keep my heart from feeling a little rejected that she seemed less than enthusiastic about moving into our home while I was gone.

CHAPTER 29

KERI

While on the return train from Chicago, I placed my rings in my reticule. As soon as I arrived home, I hurried to my room and pulled the rings out of my reticule. I rubbed my thumb over them. They were beautiful. A symbol of my marriage.

My stomach tightened over the impossible situation I created for myself. I knew I hurt James by not telling my parents immediately. I saw his slumped shoulders as he walked away.

A tear escaped from the corner of my eye. I wiped it with the back of my hand. Then I opened my jewelry box and gently laid the cherished rings inside before closing the lid.

I sat on the edge of my bed. Only it was not my bed any longer. My bed was in my husband's house.

The reality of what I did crashed in on me. I did not know how to unravel the mess I created. I flopped down on my stomach and cried.

A knock sounded on my door. "Keri, dinner is ready," Papa said.

I cleared my throat and forced a light tone. "I'll be down shortly. Just need a minute to freshen up."

When I heard his footsteps fade, I opened the door and scurried across to the washroom. Then I wet a cloth and dabbed my eyes, cheeks, and face. I hoped the red would clear from my eyes quickly.

I paused outside of the dining room. Squaring my shoulders, I pasted a smile on my face. Then I entered the room and found my usual seat. Papa bowed his head. I kept my eyes lowered when the prayer was done.

Of course, everyone asked questions about the trip. My stomach knotted again. I gave a few highlights while we dished up the meal. Then I deflected with a few strategic questions, so my siblings took over the conversation and shared what I missed while I was gone.

I barely touched my food, as my anxiety increased throughout the meal. As soon as supper finished, I retired to my room, claiming exhaustion. My lies piled one on the other.

The next day, when James stopped by the office at lunchtime, I did everything he asked of me. A chasm separated my heart from his and I hated it. I loved him, but I didn't want to disappoint my parents.

When he said he needed to travel and that he still wanted me to move into our home on Wednesday, I nearly threw up. I could not tell my parents and wanted him to do it. Instead of telling him that, I lied some more.

That afternoon at the office, I barely kept myself together. As soon as work was over, I retired to my room, feigning illness.

Finally, Wednesday came and went. I remained in my parents' home as if nothing significant changed in my life, as if I wasn't Mrs. James Colter.

At lunchtime, each day, I stopped by my husband's home to check for mail and handle anything that Maria needed. She made me lunch, which I barely ate. Then I returned to my parents' home at the end of each day.

Once I received my first letter from James, I wrote him back with heartfelt words of love, even though I avoided his questions about our home. I ignored his questions about how my parents took it. Instead, I acted like everything was fine.

After two weeks, the guilt gnawed at me. I cried at church during the music. I felt disgusted by my own actions and lies. Yet, I failed to confess the truth to anyone, least of all myself.

Then, on the third Sunday that James was gone, his mother saw me at church.

"Keri!" Hannah called to me.

"Good morning," I greeted her with a smile. "How are you doing?"

"Well. I received a letter from James, and he shared the good news." She wrapped her arms around me and squeezed tightly. "We are so glad to have you as part of the family."

I forced a smile to my lips. "Thank you. I'm so glad to be a part of the family."

"When will he be back in town?" she asked. "Will and I would love to host a reception for you when he returns."

"I… I don't know. Will you excuse me?"

I darted out of the church and ran for a block before I slowed my steps. Instead of heading home to my parents' house, I pulled my coat tighter and sat on a bench in the park. I wasn't sure how long I had sat there.

The numbness in my limbs matched the numbness in my heart. My secret and lies would be revealed. I was certain of it. Still, I could not bring myself to confess the truth.

When I could no longer feel my toes from the chill out-side, I walked home. As soon as I opened the door, Mama confronted me.

"What is going on with you, Keri? You missed Sunday supper. You aren't eating. Your dress is hanging on you. You look pale and sickly."

"I'm sorry, Mama," I mumbled. "I'm not feeling well."

"Come sit by the fire," Papa said.

I shook my head and ran upstairs to my room. Once there, I snuggled under the blanket on my bed to warm up.

A few minutes later, Papa knocked on the door.

"Go away."

He opened the door and stepped into my room. Then he closed the door and sat on the edge of my bed. He pushed my hair back from my face.

"What's going on? You've seemed out of sorts since you came back from Chicago."

Tears streamed down my face. "I don't want to talk about it."

"Did something happen between you and James? Did he hurt you?"

I shook my head. "It's nothing like that."

"Then tell me, baby girl, what's wrong?"

"I can't. I just can't."

He tried several more times, but I refused to speak. I prayed James would come home soon and fix everything for me.

CHAPTER 30

November 8, 1893

JAMES

As I rode into Prescott on my horse, the feeling that shrouded me for days was still there. I stopped at my house to drop off my things.

"Keri!" I called out when I entered.

No answer. She should have finished work for the day.

"Keri!"

I ran upstairs to my room. My heart sank. None of her things were there. The room was exactly as I left it over a month ago.

I hurried to each room, thinking she may have decided she liked another room better than the master. No sign of her or her things.

"Keri!"

"Mr. Colter!" Maria called up to me.

I hurried downstairs. "Where is Mrs. Colter?"

"I'm sorry, sir. She merely stops by at lunch each day."

I frowned. "What do you mean?"

"She never moved in, sir."

My heart broke into a thousand shards of sharp glass. I thanked Maria. Then I went into my office and searched through my important papers. I grabbed our marriage license. Then I ran out the door.

I dropped my horse off at the livery and rented a horse and wagon.

My blood boiled as I pulled the wagon to a stop in front of the Glassman home. I took the stairs on the porch in one gigantic step. Then I pounded on the door.

"James," Alex greeted. "Is something wrong?"

"I'm here to collect my wife."

I pushed past him into his house as I thrust the marriage license into his chest.

"What's this?" he asked as he unfolded the paper.

"Keri." I said her name flatly.

My heart snagged for a moment. She looked ill. She had lost weight. Her dress swallowed her frail frame. She shrank back and her tears flowed.

Alex coughed and handed the marriage license to Mel as he sank onto a chair.

"What have you done, Keri?" he asked.

Then he seemed to recover briefly. "Children, go upstairs. We need to talk to James and Keri in private."

Keri's siblings hurried away.

"Sit, James," Alex's voice was soft but commanding. I sat where I could see my wife, her parents, and her grandparents.

I crossed my arms over my chest. "Like I said, I'm here to collect my wife."

I glanced at Mel. Her face was red. Alex placed a hand over hers. He took the paper back from her. Then he stood and handed the marriage license back to me. He did not take a seat again.

"Keri?" he asked.

My jaw twitched the longer she remained silent. I cleared my throat.

"Last chance, Keri," I said. "You tell them, or I will."

She refused to look at me.

I counted to ten. Then I plowed forward.

"Keri and I eloped on September eighth, two months ago today, while we were in Chicago. The trip ended up being our honeymoon. We had a wonderful time, or at least I thought we did."

I paused and gave her a chance to say something. She remained silent.

"Nothing untoward happened," I said as my gaze connected with Alex's then Mel's. "She was eager to accept my proposal and eager to marry quickly. I did not pressure her."

"Keri," Alex said. "Is this true?"

She nodded and declined to look at any of us.

"On the train ride back, she started withdrawing. She asked me to give her a few days to tell you. We agreed she would return to live with you until that Wednesday. If she didn't tell you, the plan was that I would. Only I ended up traveling for work."

As my heart squeezed tighter, I coughed. "I take it from the shock on your faces that she never came clean."

Alex shook his head.

I said a silent prayer for wisdom. Despite my hurt and anger, Keri was my wife, and I did not want to add to the damage already done by her lies. Instead, I wanted to grab her and her things and take her home, willing to deal with the fallout later.

Yet something held me back. I thought we ought to clear the air with her family before I took her away.

"Keri," Alex said. "Look at me."

She lifted her head and did as he asked.

"The marriage license is clear. You made vows to your husband. Vows which you are not keeping."

My heart pounded against my chest.

"I…" she whispered. "I couldn't tell you."

Alex took a deep breath and kneeled in front of her chair. "I don't understand why you would find that difficult. You and I have always been close."

"I was afraid… I… Mama."

I closed my eyes to calm my racing heart.

"You can tell your mother and I anything."

She snorted and found her voice. "I can't tell Mama anything. She made her disapproval of James quite clear. I don't regret marrying James. I wanted to."

She turned her gaze toward me.

"I love him. I still want to be his wife and share my life with him."

She turned her attention toward her mother.

"But you, Mama, have been against us from the beginning. When we came back, I needed time. The longer I went saying nothing, the harder it became to tell the truth."

Her grandpa grunted. Then he slurred a word, "Leave."

I frowned. I was not leaving without my wife.

"Leave?" Maggie asked as she studied her husband's eyes.

"K-leave."

"Cleave?" she asked.

George blinked twice.

"Yes, I understand," she said.

Alex stood and took a seat next to Mel.

"George is saying 'cleave'. He wants me to remind you that when you stood before God," she paused to confirm we were married in a church.

I nodded.

"When you stood before God and vowed to love James and obey and such, your responsibility was to leave your family and cleave to your husband. Keri, you need to go with your husband. You belong with him now. It's the promise you made."

I cleared my throat as my eyes burned. I sent up a silent prayer of gratitude for George and Maggie's wisdom.

More than anything, I wanted to take my wife home. To move forward with our lives together. I would do whatever it took to repair the damage.

I settled my mind and waited for her response.

CHAPTER 31

KERI

Five pairs of eyes stared at me. My anxiety heightened to a new level. Everything they said was true. The entire situation was my fault. I knew it. I knew I hurt every one of them.

"I'm sorry," I whispered.

Then I stood and reached out for James's hand. "I'm sorry."

Tears blurred my vision. "I'm sorry I hurt you. I'm sorry I lied to you. I'm sorry that I wasn't waiting for you at home. I'm sorry that I lied and let it fester so long."

My knees gave way, and he shot to his feet to steady me.

My voice was hoarse when I spoke. "I'm so sorry, James. Please forgive… me…"

He pulled me into his arms, and I cried against his chest. At first, his hold felt stiff. Slowly, he relaxed. Eventually, he stroked my hair for a few seconds before he released me and showed me to a chair next to him.

He didn't reject me, so I breathed a sigh of relief. I had no right to expect him to forgive me so soon. I did not deserve it.

Mama cleared her throat. "I don't understand why you didn't just tell us you were married."

I straightened my back. "I didn't want you to be angry with me."

"Lying about being married is so much better?" Mama spat out the words.

"Mel," Papa warned.

"No. I need to say a few things. First, it is my right and duty to worry about you, Keri. I am your mother. Second, I'm entitled to feel angry now. Or then, if you had been honest. I can feel however I feel about what you've done. What I feel the most is disappointed."

My tears returned full force as my heart broke.

"I am disappointed that you didn't wait to get married at home in our church in front of our family. But I will agree that was your choice and James's choice to make. I'm disappointed that you lied about eloping. I'm disappointed that you cared so little—" Mama's voice cracked. "That you cared so little for your family that you lied to us. Not for days. Not for weeks, but for a month."

She let out a long breath. "I've said my peace. And I do not need a response. I just wanted you to know how hurtful your lies are."

Mama stood and marched up the stairs.

Papa turned his gaze on me. I saw his hurt and disappointment, too.

"James, what would you like to do?"

James cleared his throat. "I would like to pack up my wife's things and bring her home with me."

Papa nodded. "If you'll excuse me, I would like to go check on my wife."

James nodded.

"Keri, I would like to say goodbye before you leave. The

family will want to say farewell."

I nodded.

Papa turned and ascended the stairs.

"Come, I'll help you pack," James said.

I took his hand and led him to my room.

The silence between us felt awkward. I couldn't blame him for not wanting to say anything. Frankly, I was surprised he wanted me at all. I hated myself, so I imagined how much more he hated me.

When I opened my jewelry box, I retrieved the rings. Then I slid them onto my finger. They were looser than when I last wore them. Perhaps I lost more weight than I thought. I sighed. Then I opened my trunk and started folding my dresses.

James sighed. "I'll ask your father for a few crates."

He left, and I heard soft voices in the hallway. Then footsteps on the stairs.

By the time I finished packing my clothes, James returned with a few crates. We packed my books, jewelry box, and other belongings into the crates. I stacked my hat boxes near the door. Then I grabbed a few and headed down to the wagon waiting outside.

My brothers appeared and carried one trunk. James carried the other. I went back upstairs and retrieved a few more hat boxes. Within fifteen minutes, the four of us loaded all my things into the wagon. I followed James inside.

Papa gathered the family in the parlor. Mama held his hand.

He cleared his throat. "Everyone."

He forced a smile and tried again. "James and Keri are married now, so Keri is leaving... Our. Home."

A few tears leaked from Papa's eyes. "We wish. Them." He cleared his throat. "A long and happy life together."

My brothers and sisters stared opened-mouthed.

"Children, say your goodbyes," Mama said. "I'm sure James is exhausted after traveling all day."

Amelia came forward and gave me a big hug. "I'm gonna miss you."

"Me too."

Then Sadie cried. "I love you, sis." Then she hugged James.

Archie and Clinton hugged me but said nothing. They shook James's hand and offered him congratulations.

Then I walked to Grandma and hugged her for several seconds. Grandpa grunted and Grandma helped him to his feet. He pulled me close with his left arm. I wrapped my arms around him until he felt weak. Then I helped him sit as tears trailed down my cheeks. Tears trailed down his as well.

"I love you, too, Grandpa."

James hugged Grandma and thanked both her and Grandpa. Then he shook Grandpa's hand.

Mama stepped forward. She hugged me. "I love you, you know. I hope that you will be happy." Her voice sounded genuine.

Then she hugged James. "Welcome to the family." She placed a hand on his cheek. "We are glad to have you, despite everything."

As Papa hugged me, his shoulders shook. He stifled a sob against my hair. I cried too. Then he released me and looked into my eyes. I saw the words of love that he could not speak.

He cleared his throat and pulled James in for a hug. "Glad to have you as part of the family, James. Treat her well. I hope you'll join us for supper soon or invite us to your place. We'd love to celebrate your union."

"Thank you, Alex."

James placed his hand on the small of my back and escorted me to the waiting wagon.

When we arrived at our house, Boone waited for us. "Maria said you might need help to unpack." He hugged me. "Welcome to the family, Keri."

"Thank you."

James held the door open. He told me to sit in the parlor while he and Boone unloaded the wagon. They made quick work of it. Boone offered to return the wagon to the livery for James. We thanked him as he left.

As James closed the door, he sighed heavily.

"I… I'm not sure what to say. I am exhausted and hungry. Would you mind if we discussed this tomorrow?"

"As you wish."

"Maria!" he called the housekeeper. "We're ready to eat if you have something available."

"Yes sir. I started warming it when you came back. It will take me just a minute to set it out."

"I'm not hungry," I said.

"Bring something for Mrs. Colter anyway."

When Maria disappeared, he scolded me. "You're thin and pale. You need to eat."

"Fine." I took a seat across from him at the large cherry wood table.

Maria served us roast beef, potatoes, and carrots. I ate some of it in silence.

After supper, James led me to our room. He changed out of his clothes and climbed into bed.

"Unpack tonight if you want. Don't worry about keeping me up. I'm too tired to care."

His words stabbed my heart. Despite his comments, I tried to unpack my clothing as quietly as possible. Then I undressed and donned a nightgown. I brushed out my hair before loosely braiding it. Then I climbed into bed next to my husband. I rolled onto my side with my back facing him. After I turned down the light, I wept quietly until I fell asleep.

CHAPTER 32

JAMES

The next morning, I woke to the sound of Keri getting ready for work. I stretched and threw back the covers. Then I washed up without a word of greeting.

Her rejection of me still felt too raw. I didn't understand why she lied for so long. She loved me, I thought, and wanted to be my wife. I relaxed my jaw while I shaved. Nicking my face because of my frustration with my wife was the last thing I needed.

When I finished, I selected a dark gray suit, white shirt, and bright blue vest with matching neck scarf. I reached for a pair of cuff links. Without thinking, I grabbed the pair she gave me for my birthday. As I fastened the first one, I realized which ones I chose. My thumb ran across the eagle's head. She had called me confident. She told me I managed a crisis well. I snorted. My marriage was in a crisis, and I didn't know how to fix it.

"James," her soft voice came from the doorway. "I don't feel…"

As I turned, her body went limp and crashed to the floor. My heart lodged in my throat as I rushed to her side.

"Keri!"

I shook her, but she made no sound.

"Keri, please, love."

Nothing, save for the rise and fall of her chest as she breathed. I lifted her in my arms and laid her in our bed. My heart squeezed tight.

I ran down the stairs to Maria's quarters.

"Maria!" I knocked on her door. No answer.

Just then, the back door opened. "Mr. Colter, what's wrong?"

"Keri collapsed."

"Let me fetch the doctor," she said before she hurried out the door.

I poured a glass of water and took it back upstairs with me. I set it on the nightstand. Then I sat on the edge of the bed. I pushed her hair back from her face. Her eyes looked sunken. Her skin felt unusually dry.

My jaw tightened. I did not know how to help her.

The doctor arrived a few minutes later. He held some smelling salt under her nose. She stirred slowly.

"What happened?" she asked as she tried to sit up.

"You collapsed," I said. "The doctor is here to examine you."

"Alright."

"When did you last eat?" the doctor asked.

"I... I don't remember. Maybe Tuesday?"

I frowned as my stomach tightened. That was two days ago.

"When you did you drink something?"

"I... Don't know."

He handed her the glass of water next to the bed. "Drink all of it."

He stood and motioned me outside of the room. "She's

dehydrated and possibly malnourished. Have you noticed her not eating?"

"I just returned from traveling yesterday. She had been staying with her parents while I was gone."

"Judging by how loose her clothes are and other symptoms, I don't think she has been eating enough food. She needs to eat three wholesome meals a day. Every bite. And she needs to drink plenty of fluids, such as tea and water. Limited coffee."

I nodded. "She works at a law office in town."

"She needs to stay home until she recovers. I will come by tomorrow to check on her progress. In the meantime, even if she doesn't want to, she must eat and drink."

I showed the doctor downstairs and paid him on his way out.

"Mr. Colter, what do you need me to do?" Maria asked.

"Cook some breakfast. Once Keri eats, I will need to leave for a few hours. I'm going to the ranch. Perhaps, my mother can help for a few days."

"Yes, sir."

After Maria hurried away, I ran a hand through my hair. Keri wasn't eating. I knew she looked ill when I first saw her the previous evening. But not eating at all? I couldn't understand.

I returned upstairs and helped her down to the dining room. "The doctor said you must take time off work. You need to drink lots of water and tea, and you have to eat."

She glanced away. "I'm not hungry."

"You must eat anyway. You've made yourself sick, Keri," I said stoically.

A tear slid down her cheek. "What does it matter, anyway? You are better off without me."

My heart ripped in two. I held out a chair for her. Then

I sat and faced her. I lifted her chin with a finger. "I am not better off without you. Every word I said in that chapel in the white city, I meant, and I don't regret a single one. Am I hurt right now? Yes. But that doesn't change my commitment to you or my love for you. I want you to get better. I still want a lifetime with you by my side."

She tried to turn away, but I held her face in place. Then I brushed a gentle kiss across her lips.

Her eyes searched mine and I held her gaze.

"Alright. I'll try to eat."

Maria brought in breakfast. I took my usual seat on the other side of the table. I prayed for our meal. Then I ate my breakfast.

She picked at hers.

"Eat it," I said softly but firmly.

She did. Slowly. And she finished another glass of water.

"I'm tired. I'm going to lie down."

As she headed upstairs, I asked Maria to sit with her and ply her with more water if she didn't fall asleep.

Then I left. I headed over to the law firm. When I arrived, I asked for Alex. I would let him deliver the news to Mel as he saw fit.

Once he closed the door to his office, I started. "Keri col-lapseed this morning."

Alex coughed and stumbled into his chair. I remained standing.

"The doctor said she is malnourished and dehydrated. He thinks she has not been eating enough. When he asked her, she said she had eaten nothing since Tuesday."

Alex shook his head. "I... Something felt off with her for weeks. I tried to talk to her, but she refused to say anything. With everything that happened with George... I'm sorry."

I sighed as I gripped the back of a chair.

"She needs to gain weight and take time off work. He didn't say how long."

Alex nodded.

"Your family has a lot to worry about with George. I'll care for Keri. I'm on my way to the ranch to see if Mama can stay with us for a few days."

Alex coughed. The pain in his eyes certainly matched my own. Then he stood slowly. "Thank you, James."

I nodded and left.

As I walked to the livery to get my horse and rent a carriage, my heart felt numb. I did not know that one could be married and feel so completely alone. My heart physically beat within my chest, but all feeling ceased. That was not how I pictured the start of my marriage.

I arrived at the ranch an hour later. I pulled to a stop in front of the big ranch house. Then I knocked on the door before I opened it. The sound of typewriter keys slowed.

"Just a minute!" Ellie Mae called out from the parlor. A moment later, she entered the dining room.

"James. What happened?"

"Is Mama around?"

"After breakfast, she planned to bake at the old house."

"Thank you."

Ellie Mae reached for my arm and stopped me. "What's wrong?"

I gave her the short version of the story. She said she would pray for Keri. Then she closed the door behind me.

After I walked the horse and carriage over to the old ranch house, I knocked on the door and Mama answered.

"Mama." My voice cracked as feelings found their way into my heart again.

"James, oh, come on in."

She led me to the chair at the table. Then she poured me

some coffee.

I rarely bared my soul, but in that moment, I needed my mama more than I had in years. Then I told her the complete story and that my heart broke.

"I'm lost. I don't know what to do. Keri is sick and needs help. I love her and hate her at the same time. She confuses me and I don't know how to move forward from here."

Mama squeezed my hand. "I'll come. I'll stay for as long as you need me to."

"What about Papa and Vi?"

"Vi is old enough to cover things for me while I'm gone. Your father would want me to help you and our new daughter."

Daughter. That was just like my mama. Instantly accepting of my wife. Exactly as she had for Ellie Mae and Jaclyn, my brothers' wives.

"Go find your father and tell him what's going on. That will give me time for this pie to finish baking and to pack."

I nodded and headed toward the barn.

"James. I thought I heard someone come down the lane," Papa greeted me.

I relayed the key points of the state of my marriage and my wife's health. Ironically, the more I told the story, the less angry I was with Keri.

"I understand. I'm glad you came out for help. Hannah will know what to do."

I sighed heavily. "I don't know what to do. At my job, I know how to fix things. I don't know how to fix this."

Papa chuckled. "That's your first problem. You can't fix your wife. It's a lesson every married man must learn. The sooner you learn it, the better your marriage will be."

"I don't understand," I admitted as I ran a hand through my hair.

"A woman's heart is not a problem to be fixed. It is tender and when it is troubled, it needs careful tending. Your wife needs your comfort, your love, your prayers, your ear—listen to her—and most of all, your patience."

At that moment, I realized I had no clue what was involved in a marriage.

"Sometimes it means you take her and hold her in your arms. To her, that simple act feels like you are sheltering her from the world. Sometimes it means asking her questions to draw the words and trouble from her heart. Most of the time, it means you fall on your knees and seek wisdom from the God of Creation. He made your wife's heart, and He knows what it needs. If you let Him, He will show you the way to tend her heart."

Papa squeezed my shoulder. "Does that make sense?"

I kicked at some straw on the barn floor and stuffed my hands in my pockets. "There should be a book or manual for marriage."

Papa nodded sympathetically. "Just like you learned the railroad business on the job, the same applies to your marriage. But the Bible is as close of a manual for life, love, and relationships that I've found."

"Thank you, Papa."

He stood and walked with me to the house.

"Let me say goodbye to my wife. Then you can borrow her for as long as she thinks is wise."

Twenty minutes later, Mama rode back to town with me. Once I unloaded her things, I dropped my horse and the carriage at the livery. I stopped by the railroad to let Frank know what was going on. I promised to return to work on Friday. He understood.

When I returned, Mama and Keri sat in the dining room. I joined them.

CHAPTER 33

KERI

"Keri."

A woman's soft voice pulled me from sleep.

I opened my eyes to the kind face of my mother-in-law.

"Hannah? What are you doing here?" I sat up.

She smiled and clasped my hand. "I'm here to visit for a few days. I brought some apple pie with me. It's still warm. Would you like some?"

"I..." I wasn't hungry. I didn't want to eat.

"Well, I would like a piece. Come sit with me?"

"Alright."

I led her downstairs to the dining room. Three pieces of apple pie sat on the table. One at my seat, one at James's, and one at the head of the table.

"If you don't mind," she said, "let's not wait for James. He may be a few minutes."

When I sat down, the aroma of fresh baked apple pie made my mouth water. I supposed I could try to eat a few bites.

Hannah smiled before she ate a bite of the pie. She laughed. "I always let the boys think I made pie just for them. I wanted them to feel as special as they are. Sometimes the pie was really just for me."

I swallowed a bite of pie, then I smiled. "Your secret is safe with me."

"I was glad to hear that the railroad business is picking up again. I know how much it means to James. He needed the time off with you, too."

The first bite of pie did not satiate my taste buds, so I took another. Sweetness faded to tartness as I chewed the warm pie.

"I know he loves you very much."

I frowned. "How do you know that?"

"He's told me. James hardly tells me anything, but he told me that. He told me before you left for Chicago that he planned to propose to you."

I ate another bite of pie. "He did?"

"He planned it carefully. He thought he might take you on a gondola ride and propose, then."

I smiled softly. "We rode the gondola, but that was the evening of our wedding. It was so peaceful and beautiful." I sighed. "I snuggled up against him and he wrapped his arm around me. As the sun set, the electric lights cast reflections on the water. It was one of the most beautiful things I've ever seen."

"Not as beautiful as you on our wedding day."

James's voice came from behind me. He placed a hand on my shoulder. Then he leaned down to kiss my cheek.

My cheeks warmed as memories of our wedding night came to mind.

"Mama, is this for me?" he asked as he sat across from me.

"Of course. Though if you were gone much longer, I considered eating it."

"You wouldn't?" he teased.

She laughed. "We will never know."

I smiled at their banter. For the first time since arriving at James's house, it felt a little like mine, too.

"Would you like another piece, Keri?" Hannah asked.

I looked down at my empty plate. "Oh, I shouldn't. We haven't had lunch yet."

She winked at me. "I'm sure it would be fine, just this once."

"I'll pass."

"Alright. Let me just take our plates to the kitchen." She took my plate away before I could remind her that Maria would do that.

"It's good to see your smile," James said. "I missed you while I was gone. Thank you for writing to me. It made the separation more bearable."

"Of course. I loved receiving your letters."

Hannah and Maria entered the dining room with sandwiches for lunch. Hannah set a plate in front of me. Then she took her seat again.

"Tell me all about your wedding and the fair," she said.

I took a bite of my sandwich as James told the story of our wedding day.

"I need to have a word with your brothers," she said. "Make sure they know I would like to be invited to their weddings."

She winked at me.

"Though as long as they end up with the woman God intends for them, I won't complain."

———

Hannah stayed with us for a few days and returned

home on Sunday after church. I was grateful for her help. She helped James and I fall into normal and loving conversation again without us realizing it. She encouraged me to eat in such a disarming way. The time I cherished the most was while James went to work on Friday, she helped me clear my conscience with God and myself.

When we returned home from church on Sunday, I knew it was time to talk to James. We sat on the couch in the parlor, staring into the fire. His arm rested on my shoulders. I leaned against his chest.

"James," I started and kept my gaze fixed on the fire. Somehow, it made the words easier to speak. "Please forgive me for not honoring you in so many ways. My parents should have been told immediately. I was wrong to ask you to let me have a few days. I was wrong to lie to you and them."

I sat upright and turned my head so I could see his face. He kept his arm lightly around my shoulders.

"I forgive you. I don't understand why you did it, but I forgive you."

His fingers trailed along my cheek.

"I'm not sure I understand why I did it. Initially, I was so afraid of upsetting my mother and disappointing my parents. I couldn't see how upside down my priorities were. I should have put you first. You were right to ask that of me and I failed you."

My eyes burned. "As the days rolled on, my lies multiplied, and I felt trapped in a cell of my making. If I could do it over, I'd go home with you and work to repair any perceived harm my parents felt."

As I searched his dark brown eyes, I took his face in my hands. "I never stopped loving you, even when I acted in such an unloving way. James, you are my life and my love. I want many years of laughter and happiness with you."

His eyes reddened. Then he pulled me into a tight hug. He clung to me and I to him. After some length of time, he loosened his hold and lifted my face to his. His lips tenderly swept across mine. I leaned into him, and his kiss deepened. Then he stopped and led me to our room, where we found forgiveness and healing in each other's arms.

———

In the early evening, James left my side. I donned a nightgown and climbed back into bed. I rolled over to take a nap, but there was a soft knock on the door. James opened it carrying a tray with food.

He beamed. "You've heard of breakfast in bed. Well, how about supper in bed?"

I sat up and smiled. I pulled my hair to one side as he set a tray of sandwiches and fruit in front of me. My gaze traveled up to his eyes.

"Why are you so kind to me? I don't deserve this."

He snorted as he pulled a chair near the bed. "None of us do."

I frowned as he sighed heavily.

"Foremost, you are my wife. I love you, and we can't have a long and loving marriage if I hold on to bitterness and refuse to forgive you, can we?"

I shook my head as I reached for a sandwich. I took a bite. Maria was an excellent cook.

"Second, I know what it is like to have someone refuse to forgive me."

"I have a hard time believing someone wouldn't forgive you, James. You are the most honorable and decent man that I know."

"Thank you." He smiled. "You might be a little biased."

I laughed. "Of course, I am. Tell me who won't forgive you."

He took a sandwich and leaned back in the chair. After he swallowed, he answered me. "Sam. Sam is still angry with me because I ran the SFP&P through a tiny, useless corner of his land."

As I finished the last bite of my sandwich, I sipped on the tea he brought up for me. My mind worked through the problem.

At length, I said, "It sounds like we both need to seek reconciliation with some family members."

"Yes. We need a plan."

"Do you think he and Ellie Mae would accept a dinner invitation from us?"

James wiped some crumbs from his lap. "I don't know."

"What if I extended the invitation through Ellie Mae?"

"That might work. I think she wants to see the two of us speaking again."

"Then I shall invite them for supper after church next week. Perhaps your mother and sister could watch their children to give us time without distractions?"

"I'm certain they would." He cleared his throat. "Now, what about your family?"

I let out a long breath. "I suppose I should invite them for supper. Does Friday evening work?"

He nodded.

"Should I invite just my parents?"

He grabbed another sandwich and considered the idea. He nodded to the sandwiches and to me. I took a second one.

"I think it would be wise to start with your parents. Thanksgiving is soon, so that will be an opportunity to see your entire family if we are going to your house for the day."

"Do you think your family would host my family for Thanksgiving?"

"I can ask Mama about it." He wiggled his eyebrows. "At work when Frank and I have a new project, but we don't want anyone to know what we are talking about, we give it a code name. We should give this plan a code name."

I laughed. "Like what?"

"Rose buds."

I chuckled. "Why rose buds?"

"They are the first visible sign of something beautiful about to bloom. I think if we reconcile with all our family members, it will be the beginning of something rather beautiful."

After sipping more tea, I agreed wholeheartedly. "Rose buds it is."

"Now, if you've had enough supper, I'll set the tray outside for Maria." He gave me that come hither look of his. "I'd like to cuddle with my wife."

CHAPTER 34

JAMES

I didn't tell my wife that project Rose Buds included working out a job for her. I knew she wanted to go back to work, and I still wanted her at the railway.

The last time the doctor stopped by, he thought she looked significantly healthier. She put on some much-needed weight and ate regularly without fussing. The color returned to her face.

Yet she was antsy. If she desired to stay home, I'd not press for her to go to work. But I knew her heart and that a career fulfilled her dreams.

"Good morning, Frank," I greeted him on Monday morn-ing when I entered his office.

"How is Daniel doing with his new role?" he asked.

"Excellent. He has always made good decisions." I was proud of Daniel Parker. In the few short weeks as the Vice President of Transportation, my old job, he excelled. He brought fresh ideas to the role.

I cleared my throat. "Now that we are back on track financially, I think it is time to bring back a few key roles."

Frank eyed me. "Such as?"

"A contract attorney."

"Your wife," he said flatly.

"Yes. May I remind you she saved us thousands of dollars in three short weeks?"

Frank drummed his fingers on the table.

"She proved that there is a need for the position."

He sighed. "You will not let this go, will you?"

I smiled and shook my head.

"Why can't your wife get involved with charitable work?" he muttered. Then he sighed. "Fine. She can start after Thanksgiving."

I grinned.

With the closure of Bullock's line while I was in Congress at the end of October, we were free to charge competitive and profitable rates again. An influx of investment capital also improved our standing. We were once again able to focus our time and energy on future expansion, like project Marco Polo.

We spent the next hour strategizing about the project. Frank named it after the famous explorer who opened up trade with the East and Asia. It was for a new eastern spur that would start north of Granite Dells and head east toward Mayer and beyond.

As I headed home, I stopped at the flower shop and purchased a bouquet for my wife. With the refrigerated cars on the rail lines, we received fresh flowers often enough to support such a shop. I planned to make use of it frequently.

"Keri!" I called out as I opened the door.

She approached the entryway from the parlor. Her eyes lit with pleasure and surprise as I handed her the flowers.

"Thank you. They are lovely."

"I thought you might like some good news to go with the flowers."

"Oh?"

"Frank has agreed that you can come back to the SFP&P after Thanksgiving."

She launched herself into my arms. I hugged her tight and twirled her around before setting her down. She kept her arms around my neck.

"Truly?"

I smiled. "I take it you're pleased?"

She placed a big kiss on my lips. "More than pleased."

"Good," I said as I released her.

"Thank you, James."

She entered the kitchen for a vase and water. When she returned and arranged the flowers, I stood in the doorway of the dining room and studied her.

My papa's advice was spot on. In tending to her heart, loving her, and forgiving her, my wife seemed to return to normal. In some ways, our hearts grew even closer together. I would have to thank Papa the next time I saw him. I don't know that I would have figured it out on my own.

She glanced up and smiled. "I hope these last through the weekend. It would be nice to have the flowers for supper with my parents and then with your brother and Ellie Mae."

"I can always buy more, if you'd like."

"Ellie Mae was in at the Gazette today, so she found my note and stopped by," Keri said.

"Oh?"

"She said that she and Sam would be delighted to join us after church on Sunday. She will ask Vi to watch the children. I just hope she doesn't have her baby while she is here. She's huge."

I snorted and shook my head. That would be Sam's fourth child. I had some catching up to do.

CHAPTER 35

KERI

Friday arrived sooner than I was ready. James and I spent every morning praying over our planned meal with my parents. I wanted them to forgive me, especially Mama. I wanted her to understand that neither James nor I meant to cause harm or to disappoint her.

When James arrived home early from the office, he held a lovely bouquet in his hand. I kissed him on the cheek and changed out the flowers on the table to the fresh ones. My hands shook, and he noticed.

"Hey," he said as he came to stand next to me. "Everything will be alright. Your parents love you. They will want to reconcile as much as we do."

I let out a shaky breath. "I don't know why I'm so afraid of my mother's disappointment."

He smiled. "It's alright. Tonight is about asking for forgiveness and moving on. If your mother holds on to disappointment, that is on her, not on us."

"I know."

"Why don't we start by showing them around the house? That will be a good way to start the conversation about something that neither of us finds too personal."

"Yes, that would be nice," I said as I dropped the last carnation into the vase.

At precisely six o'clock, my parents arrived. I hugged Papa first, then Mama. They both shook James's hand.

"Would you care to see the house?" James asked.

"Love to," Papa said.

Mama seemed nervous to me as James led us through the tour. When we climbed the stairs, Mama let out a sigh.

"So many rooms," she said.

"I was thinking this one," I said, pointing to the smallest of the bedrooms, "would be a pleasant room for the nanny since it adjoins the room next to it."

When Mama's eyes widened, I hastened to add, "Not that we have need of it yet."

"I agree," James said. "I always envisioned it as such."

"It's lovely," Mama said.

James led us back down to the dining room. When we entered, Mama smiled.

"It's lovely."

I held back a snicker. Seemed Mama's vocabulary was stuck on one word.

"Looks like it would accommodate the entire family if you were to host a holiday meal," Papa said.

"I would like that," I said. "The Colters invited us, including the Glassmans, out to the ranch for Thanksgiving."

Papa's face lit with excitement. "Really?"

James nodded. "If George feels up to it, we can bring him and Maggie out. Mama and Ellie Mae already promised a noon-time meal so we will have plenty of time to visit and return home before dark."

Mama smiled. "That would be nice. His health seems to improve each day. He's been able to grasp a fork with his right hand again."

"Oh, how wonderful!" I exclaimed as James showed them to their seats.

"These dishes are quite—"

"Lovely?" I asked.

Mama chuckled. "I suppose I have overused the word. How about beautiful?"

I nodded as I ran a finger along the gold stripe on the edge of a plate. "James and I picked them out last week. I thought they were sophisticated yet simple."

"Would you care for some wine?" James asked. Both my parents accepted. He just finished pouring the wine when Maria set out the food.

The conversation flowed while we enjoyed the roast duck. I relaxed and my parents seemed to, as well. They talked about news of my siblings and the law office.

"After Thanksgiving, I'll work at the railway again," I said. "James convinced Frank that they couldn't live without me."

"Congratulations," Papa said with a genuine smile.

As soon as supper was over, we retired to the parlor, where James got down to business.

"First," he said, "I would like to apologize for not asking your permission for Keri to marry me."

Papa sighed and clasped Mama's hand. She kept her face impassive. "I was a little hurt, but not overly surprised. It was obvious the two of you wanted to marry. I appreciate the apology."

"I would also like to apologize for not telling you both that we eloped as soon as we returned to Prescott. As the leader of my family, I failed to lead well. Then the burden fell on my wife and caused everyone undue stress."

Papa's gaze connected with mine. I gave him a tentative

smile. He knew I was as much to blame as James, even though I appreciated James trying to take the weight from me.

"I owe you an apology as well," I said. "I should have never tried to convince James to hide the truth. Even though he compromised with me, I should have told you both the truth immediately. I'm sorry."

Mama cleared her throat. "I must apologize for being overly critical of both of you. I see now that if I had been more gracious and accepting of your relationship, perhaps you would not have felt the need to hide it."

I stood and rushed to Mama to hug her. "Mama, I forgive you," I said through my tears. "I just want us to move for-ward. Both of you should be frequent visitors to our house."

Papa stood and hugged me. "We want nothing more. Well, maybe some grandchildren might be nice."

James laughed. "I'm sure we can arrange that."

We all laughed, and the conversation moved on. We restored our relationship with my parents.

Our next challenge was Sam.

CHAPTER 36

JAMES

I paced the length of our room while I waited for Keri to finish fixing her hair before church on Sunday.

"James, calm down."

"I am calm."

She laughed. "No, you aren't. You're wearing a rut in the floor."

When I stopped pacing, I ran a hand through my hair.

"It will be fine. We've prayed over this. I truly believe Sam will come around. He can't avoid you forever. Nor will Ellie Mae let him."

She patted a hand to her head. "There. I'm ready."

I grabbed my walking stick and offered her my arm. Then we strode to church on time. As we neared the building, I saw my family gathered outside.

After I greeted Mama, she hugged me and whispered in my ear, "All will be well."

I hoped she was right. The rift between my brother and me exhausted me.

Keri greeted Ellie Mae and Sam. Then we all entered the building for the service. I fidgeted the entire time, and I about drove my wife mad.

As soon as the service finished, I led the way home. Keri walked next to Ellie Mae, so that left Sam by my side.

"I'm sorry Sam. I do hope you will forgive me for running the railroad through Colter land."

Sam snorted. "And for going around me to the legislature to do it?"

I sighed. It was not going well. Perhaps I should have waited until after we ate.

"We failed to work it out on our own. I did what I needed to do."

"Sam," Ellie Mae said his name with a warning tone. I wasn't sure she and Keri were listening until that moment.

Sam sighed. "It hurt that you would take legal action against your own brother. I never imagined you would. I wanted you to fight for our family more than your railroad."

I frowned. "Don't you see? The railroad was fighting for our family and hundreds of other families in town. Our railroad provides a way to ship goods from Prescott across the country. As the line finishes to Phoenix next year, it will open more opportunities. One of those opportunities is for you to sell cattle easily far beyond the local area. You can increase your herd size and increase your profits long term."

I held the door open as they entered. Then I continued, "It also brings goods to town from other places. Everyone benefits from our line. So, do I regret slicing off a small corner of Colter land? No."

I cleared my throat. "However, I do regret that it has caused so much animosity in our relationship. You are my brother. We grew up together. You and I were as close as Deacon and Grady when we were younger, and I want us to be friends again."

"Sam!" Ellie Mae cried out as she gripped the back of a

chair. "Oh, no, no, no."

Keri held her other hand. "Is it time?"

Ellie Mae screamed while she nodded her head.

"Sam," Keri said. "The doctor. The baby is coming."

Sam's face went white. His feet locked in place. I tugged on his arm.

"Go! We'll go upstairs to one of the guest rooms. You get the doctor."

Keri and I helped Ellie Mae up to the guest room closest to the stairs. Then I returned downstairs for Maria, who flew into a flurry of activity. She handed me a nightgown. My face heated hotter than burning coals as I took the garment upstairs. My wife snatched it from my hand and shooed me out of the room.

A few minutes later, Sam returned with the doctor. I showed them upstairs. Then I headed for the parlor to wait. What a disaster of an afternoon.

After an hour, Sam joined me in the parlor. "It will be a while yet. I'm sorry the baby is coming at your house."

I offered him some brandy, and he accepted. Then I asked Maria to bring in some food. When she did, I offered it to Sam.

"Are you hungry? Have something to eat."

He shook his head while he sipped the brandy.

"I should be used to this by now," he muttered, "with it being our fourth child." He held up the glass. "I might start a new tradition with this. It helps me relax some."

Loud screams came from the upstairs room. I set my plate of food aside, no longer hungry.

"Is this what it's like?" I asked. "Hours of this?"

He nodded. "The worst part is feeling so completely helpless."

I started a fire in the fireplace. We both sat in silence for some length of time.

"I forgive you, James, and I'm sorry I've held a grudge for so long. I understand why you did it."

I glanced at him as he stared into the fire.

"I guess I just wanted you to acknowledge what you did. You have done that and now I have acknowledged my part in it, too."

I offered him more brandy. He accepted.

"To the Colter brothers!" I raised my glass. He clanked his glass on mine. "May we always be friends and put our differences behind us."

"Here, here."

We both took a sip. I sat down again and waited with my brother for the birth of his new child.

"Sam!" Keri called from the top of the stairs. "Come meet your new son."

Sam bounded up the stairs two at a time. I followed at a more leisurely pace.

"Is Ellie Mae alright?" I asked as I joined my wife in the hallway.

"She is just fine. Exhausted. Both mother and son are healthy."

I clasped Keri's hand. "Did you have any idea giving birth takes so long?"

She laughed. "Mama was in labor with Amelia for twenty hours."

I felt the blood drain from my face. Keri put her arms around me.

"Don't you pass out, James. I don't think I can carry you."

"I…" I shook it off. "I'm fine."

"James," Sam said. "Come in and meet your nephew, Riley."

I entered the room and offered my congratulations to Ellie Mae and Sam. Then Sam stood and held out his son. "Do you want to hold him?"

I backed up a step, but Keri was behind me, blocking my way.

"Come," Sam invited. He showed me how to support the baby's head and neck.

"I don't want to break him." My heart pounded as my little nephew settled into my arms.

"You're doing great," Keri said. "A natural."

Riley seemed so tiny in my arms. He cooed as I rocked him back and forth. My heart melted.

"Such a handsome man. I think you take after your uncle."

Sam laughed. "Deacon will be pleased to hear it."

I smirked at him.

When he fussed, Keri took little Riley from my arms, and she handed him to his mama.

"We'll leave you. If you need anything, ask," she said before she pushed me out of the room.

We returned to the parlor, and I asked Maria to bring food for Keri. Then we sat on the couch and stared into the fire. It seemed to be our tradition on Sunday evenings, even though that one was in a class of its own.

She nibbled on a sandwich as she settled against my chest.

"How did you know what to do?" I asked. "You seemed like a natural mother. Well, aunt."

She laughed. "I was nine when Amelia was born. Grandma helped Mama, and she asked me to watch. I think she saw it as an opportunity for me to learn."

"I was the oldest, but I honestly don't remember a single birth. One day, there was a new baby in the house. I don't know if I'm ready for this—for it to be you."

My eyes burned as I thought of all the things that could go wrong.

"James, don't borrow trouble from tomorrow. When my time comes, Grandma, Mama, and your mother will all support me. It wouldn't surprise me if my sisters, Jaclyn, or Ellie Mae would help as well."

I snorted. "I definitely need more brandy on hand. Sam finally relaxed after the second glass."

Keri smiled. "I'll make sure Maria sees to it when the time comes."

My stomach knotted as I worried how things would go for her despite all her reassurances.

CHAPTER 37

KERI

On Thanksgiving, I woke early to help Ellie Mae. James, and I drove out the day before and stayed overnight at Grandma's old house. I knew Ellie Mae would need as much help as she could get with a newborn and hosting the large family meal.

Hannah was already buzzing around the kitchen by the time I entered the ranch house.

"Breakfast is on the table," she said. "I'm letting everyone serve themselves as they show up."

I grabbed a few slices of bacon and some eggs. I hurried to finish them before I offered my help.

"Where do you need me?"

"Peeling potatoes?"

"You've got it."

I sat at the table and peeled potatoes until my hands hurt. "How many people are we expecting again?"

"Goodness. I've lost count," Hannah said. "All my boys and their families, except Preston. Then Grady and his new bride. Your entire family."

"Mama," Vi said as she breezed into the dining room.

"Papa thinks it's going to be nice enough that we can set up tables outside. What do you think?"

"I suppose so. There's really not enough room in here for everyone."

"I noticed Grandma's table and chairs are still over at her place," I said. "Perhaps we could use those too?"

"Vi, ask Deacon and Grady to handle it."

I smiled at my mother-in-law's command of the situation. She had everything perfectly under control. I helped with several other dishes, grateful that Grandma taught me the basics of cooking, even though I rarely practiced.

By eleven o'clock, we set several tables up in the yard with a lovely view of the lake. One table was in the shade of a large tree for Grandpa and the newborn Riley.

As I carried some mashed potatoes out to the table where Grandpa sat, I greeted him with a big hug. "I'm so glad you felt up to coming."

"Good. Here," he said. The left side of his mouth turned up in a half smile. I could see the joy in his eyes.

"I'm sure it feels good to be home for a while."

"Yes."

My heart warmed to see how much he improved and that he spoke several basic words.

I greeted my parents, siblings, and Grandma before I went back into the ranch house to grab more food. When I stepped onto the porch, James took the food from me. I turned and retrieved more.

Once we set out everything, Will stood and offered a blessing. Then we passed food around.

"I am thankful for," Vi started, "more new sisters at last!"

I laughed, knowing they counted me as one of them.

"I am thankful for," Sam said, "my older brother James and his help the day Riley was born."

James laughed. "And I'm thankful that Riley looks more like his mama than his papa." James squeezed Sam's shoulder as he said the words.

Everyone laughed.

When it was my turn, I paused for a moment. "I am thank-ful for the honeymoon suite at the Congress Plaza Hotel."

James chuckled, as he knew the hidden meaning behind my words.

"And of course, for my handsome husband and our great families," I added.

Others shared what they were thankful for. Then it was Grandma and Grandpa's turn. Grandma stood.

"George and I are thankful for all of you and the tremendous help you've been over the last few months. We are overjoyed to visit the ranch for the day. May God bless our families for generations to come."

Grandpa added, "Amen."

Everyone clapped and cheered before returning to their food.

When we finished our meal, James rested his arm on the chair behind me. Then he whispered so only I could hear.

"I'm the most thankful for you, my love. I'm thankful you agreed to be my wife and are healthy again. We overcame some difficult times with the help of God and our families."

I leaned against him, and he held me close.

"I'm thankful for you, James. That you chose me for that dance two years ago. That you invited me on a train ride before you burned down a town."

He snorted.

"That you never stopped loving me, even when I hurt you so."

I turned my face toward him.

"And that you invited me to be a part of the railroad."

He leaned closer and captured my lips with his for a brief kiss. When he pulled away, I thought no one noticed, until I heard Grandpa's laughter.

"That. My. Girl."

EPILOGUE

Prescott, Arizona Territory
August 20, 1894

JAMES

I sipped on my second brandy as my wife labored to deliver our first child. I thought I was nervous when my nephew was born. But that was nothing compared to listening to my wife.

Another scream came from upstairs. My heart tore at each one.

"Take a breath, son," Papa said. "It will be alright. Your mother has everything under control."

I sipped my brandy, glad that my parents came out to stay with us for a few days. Mama seemed to know exactly how to time the visit, as they only arrived earlier that morning.

Papa placed his hand on my shoulder. Then he whispered a prayer for my wife, my child, and me. I was still a nervous wreck and thought I would be until I could see her again.

Then the cries of a newborn echoed through the house.

I set my brandy down on the side table and darted to my feet.

"Give them a minute," Papa warned.

I paced back and forth until Mama called down to me.

"James, come meet your son."

I ran up the stairs and nearly tripped on the top step. Then I hurried into the room. Tears burned my eyes when I caught sight of my weary wife smiling down at our son. I sniffed.

"Tate Alexander Colter, say hi to your papa."

Papa. The word hit my chest like a ton of bricks. I thought I was ready, yet the word terrified me.

I sat on the edge of the bed and wrapped an arm around my wife. Then I leaned in and touched his cheek with my fingers.

"Hello, Tate," I said before emotion clogged my throat.

"He's perfect, James," Keri said. "Oh, I love him so much already."

Then, I felt it too. Overwhelming love for my tiny son.

I ripped my eyes away from him for a minute to study my wife. She smiled at me.

"And you? You are alright?"

"I am. Would you like to hold him?"

I nodded.

Then she placed our son in my arms. I leaned down and kissed his forehead. My boy. Another generation of Colters. I wondered if he would grow up to be an attorney like his mother, or a rancher like his grandpa. Or a railroad magnate like me.

"I see that look," Keri teased, before she yawned.

"What?"

"You've already mapped out his career and probably married him off. He's not even an hour old yet."

I winked at her. "If he's going to be a railroad man, we need to start him early."

Then we laughed as love filled our hearts to overflowing.

AUTHOR'S NOTE

For years, I've wanted to write about the railroads in Arizona. As I thought about James Colter's story, I knew from the beginning that I wanted him to be a pivotal part of the railroad. So, I started researching and reading everything I could find about the railroads. His birthdate was set in stone since it was already recorded in the *Prescott Pioneer's Series*. I knew I had to pick a railroad that fit with his age in the 1880's and 1890's. This was the main motivation in writing his story as book 3, even though he was the firstborn Colter son.

When I discovered the book *The Santa Fe, Prescott, and Phoenix Railway: The Scenic Line of Arizona* by John W. Sayre, I struck gold. John's book was a very detailed and well-researched account of the now defunct railroad. He also wrote about the railroad wars between Thomas Bullock's Central Arizona Railway and the Santa Fe, Prescott, and Phoenix Railway.

James Colter is a figment of my imagination. However, several of the other minor characters related to the railroads were how I imagined some real people may have acted. Thomas Bullock, Frank Murphy, and D.B. Robinson were all real people involved with the railroads in the way I described in this book.

Also, all the dates mentioned about the railroads came

straight from Sayre's book, from the incorporation of the SFP&P on May 25, 1891, to the inaugural trip on April 24, 1893, to the date that D.B. Robinson stepped down as president on October 9, 1893. Bullock's line ceased operation on October 21, 1893. Had his line continued on, there was a strong likelihood that both lines would have gone under, since Prescott was not large enough to support two railroad lines.

The number of employees laid off after the financial crises of 1893 is an estimate based on the number of employees listed as required for construction of the southern part of the line. The actual labor cost of $500 per month was accurate. So was the $8 million capital outlay and the requirement by the A&P to hold 51% of the capital in a fund for investors for five years after the end of construction.

The one historical fact that I took liberty with was the fire in Ash Fork. I came across multiple accounts of a fire in Ash Fork that demolished the entire town. However, I was never able to pin down the exact date. The best I could tell by cross-referencing different facts, was that the fire actually took place sometime between August 1893 and December 1893. The station in Ash Fork was not completed until the fall of 1893. The accounts of the fire mentioned the depot burned to the ground, so that is why I'm guessing the real fire was in the later part of the year. I chose to place the fire at the time of the inaugural trip (April 24, 1893) to add tension to the story and amplify James's feelings for Keri.

I really enjoyed finding ways to incorporate the real-life story of this railway that made a lasting impression on Prescott.

The love story between James and Keri is perhaps my favorite story to date. I am sure you may have been wondering how I was going to wrap up their story when I chose to write their elopement around the two-thirds mark in the book. I really wanted to show an example of a marriage that started out with some obstacles to overcome. I wanted to show how a godly man might handle a huge curve ball from his new, parent-pleasing bride. It also gave me the opportunity to show, yet again, what kind of father Will Colter was.

I also enjoyed writing the relationship between Keri and her father, Alex. When I first developed Alex's character in *Oaks of Justice*, I finished the story describing how much Keri was like him. So, in *The Railroad Magnate*, I pushed that relationship to the limit. I love that Alex loved his firstborn daughter so deeply and that her gender never mattered to him.

Anyway, I hope you enjoyed James and Keri's story. Con-tinue the story with Deacon Colter and Grady Thatcher, in *The Resourceful Stockman (Colter Sons Book 4)*.

Karen Baney

Want More Arizona Territory Romance?

Get a FREE novella featuring characters connected to the Colter Sons series! Plus exclusive updates on new releases, special offers, and historical insights from the frontier.

Subscribe at: books.karenbaney.com/larson-christmas

ABOUT THE AUTHOR

Karen Baney is passionate about writing stories full of flawed characters. She enjoys weaving together stories of second chances, redemption, and overcoming personal trials. As a transplant to Arizona, she loves researching the state's history and finding ways to seamlessly incorporate real history and real settings into her novels. In addition to writing and speaking, Karen works as a Software Development Manager for a Christian ministry.

Her faith plays an important role both in her life and in her writing. Karen and her husband, Jim, make their home in Gilbert, Arizona, with their two dogs, Bella and Daisy. Both Jim and Karen are active at Rock Point Church in Queen Creek, Arizona.

Discover faith-laced stories with characters who feel like lifelong friends.

Visit www.karenbaney.com to discover more historical romance series set in the American West. Follow Karen's writing journey and get behind-the-scenes glimpses of her research adventures on social media.

Facebook: @AuthorKarenBaney
X: @karen_baney
Instagram: @AuthorKarenBaney
BookBub: Follow Karen Baney for new release alerts

BOOKS BY KAREN BANEY

Historical Western Romance

Prescott Pioneers Series:
Step back in time to the wild, untamed Arizona Territory where survival depends on grit, faith, and the courage to start over. Follow three pioneer families—the Andersons, Colters, and Larsons—as they risk everything for the promise of a new life in a land that demands both strength and hope.

A Dream Unfolding
A Heart Renewed
A Life Restored
A Hope Revealed
Hidden Prospects

Desert Manna Series:
Sometimes the most beautiful love stories bloom in the desert. Set in the growing frontier town of Prescott during the early 1870s, these tender romances follow women rebuilding their lives after heartbreak and the unexpected men who help them discover that second chances at love are worth the risk. Set in Prescott, Arizona between 1871 - 1873.

Beauty for Ashes
Joy for Mourning
Oaks of Justice

Colter Sons Series:
Power, legacy, and forbidden love collide in this sweeping family saga set in the Arizona Territory. The Colter ranch

empire has weathered decades of frontier life, but now family secrets and buried betrayals threaten to destroy everything. As five brothers—and one resilient sister—navigate the treacherous waters of love, loss, and redemption, they must decide what's worth fighting for. Set in Prescott and other locations within the Arizona Territory in 1887 - 1906."

The Reluctant Cattleman
The Roaming Adventurer
The Railroad Magnate
The Resourceful Stockman
The Restless Wrangler
The Resilient Bride

Larson Sisters Series
Meet the next generation! These delightful novellas follow the three daughters of Adam and Julia Larson from the *Prescott Pioneers Series* as they navigate love, courtship, and finding their own happily ever afters in territorial Arizona in 1886 – 1894.

In Love at Christmas
In Love with the Rancher
In Love with the Horse Trainer

Contemporary Romance

Vargas Ranch Series:
Love is in the air at the Vargas Guest Ranch & Resort near Wickenburg, Arizona. Meet the Vargas family—five swoon-worthy brothers and their cousins who live by their family motto: "We do not deviate from the Lord's plan."

These rugged cowboys run a successful working ranch and luxury resort while navigating the rollercoaster of finding true love.

Falling for a Fake Cowboy
Falling for a Real Cowboy
Honeymoon with a Real Cowboy
Falling for a Shy Cowboy
Falling for a Bossy Cowboy
Falling for a Smart Cowboy
Falling for a Humbug Cowboy
Falling for a Devoted Cowgirl
Falling for a Pregnant Cowgirl
Falling for a Cowboy's Legacy

Steadfast Love Series:

The *Steadfast Love* series follows a close-knit group of friends as they navigate the beautiful mess of modern life in the Phoenix area—workplace drama, complicated families, and love that shows up when they least expect it. These contemporary romances blend emotional depth with authentic faith, reminding us that even when life unravels, God's love never does.

The Heart I Rescue (prequel)
The Air I Breathe

I never expected to lose my heart to someone connected with the crime.

My best friend's parents were murdered…

Now he needs my help.

My name is Deacon Colter. My best friend's parents were murdered. To help him, I must overcome the worst of my obsessive-compulsive nature.

While on the trail of the rustlers and murderers, I meet a woman who pique's my interest. There's only one impossible problem: it's her father we're hunting down.

Is she involved? Can I trust her?

Even leaning on the Lord, I don't have the answers. I never expected 1893 to tear my world apart.

———

If you love emotionally rich Christian romance with rugged frontier grit...

Janette Oke meets Louis L'Amour. Mary Connealy meets Zane Grey.

The *Colter Sons* series blends heartfelt faith journeys, masculine coming-of-age arcs, and sweeping Arizona history into unforgettable love stories.

DESERT LIFE MEDIA

———

Desert Life Media: *There Is Life in The Desert*

Entertainment-first Christian fiction set in the Southwest, featuring redemption, family, and faith

Publishing clean, wholesome, and uplifting fiction since 2010

———

desertlifemedia.com